RADIANT
NighT

RADIANT Night

PATRICK LOHIER

ADAPTIVE BOOKS

An Imprint of Adaptive Studios
Los Angeles, CA

Visit us on the web at www.adaptivestudios.com

Library of Congress Cataloging in Publication Number: 2018942295
ISBN 978-1-945293-66-5
Ebook ISBN 978-1-945293-67-2

Printed in the United States of America
Designed by Elyse J. Strongin, Neuwirth & Associates

Adaptive Books
3733 Motor Avenue
Los Angeles, CA 90034

10 9 8 7 6 5 4 3 2 1

For my parents.
And for Sree, Om and Sai.

RADIANT
NighT

0.

Ludwig Mason shoots into the sky. Up, up, up he soars as smoke trails from his ass like ash from the tail of a reborn phoenix. At first it feels like falling, only upside down, a nightmare. But after all the months of *hurryup* . . . and w a i t . . . *hurryup* and w a i t . . . he discovers that he's able to ease into it, this strange sensation, and after all the crap that's been going on for days down below, he starts to find the silence and solitude kind of comforting, like an unexpected stretch of R&R.

The Humvee he was riding crashes to the road beneath him.

The driver of the Humvee, erstwhile, one big, quiet former high school wrestler named Pete "Wonder" McCowan, late of Lewiston, Vermont, is torn apart. His blond head, his sunburned face, his green eyes, his gum-chewing, whiskey-swilling, pussy-lapping mouth—the seat of everything he's ever known and felt—hurtles through the driver's-side window and tumbles a yard or two into the field south of the road, a field tufted with patches of tenacious beige grass that

Ludwig, for months now, has noticed somehow find a footing in that dust. It takes a few minutes for the rest of Wonder's body to burn and sink into his seat's twisted metal frame, leaving a charred mass like a roast left in the oven for far too long.

In the backseat, gentle, soft-spoken Rick Ferrer, of Cochran, Arizona, knows a brief flash of terror before he, too, is shattered by the blast. Most of his body remains on the bench on which he sits, but some of him—some hair and skin and bone gristle from his neck and shoulders—blows out, shredded, fused, and intermingled with the minuscule cubes of ballistic-resistant window glass that rain down on the road for yards behind the blast.

And riding shotgun is the biggest bastard, the biggest badass that ever was and likely ever will be in the corps: Hugh Vance, of Almota, Washington, six-foot-four, their might, their muscle, a fucking straight-out-of-the-box, anatomically super-correct superhero. The force of the explosion splits Vance in half. His legs and hips stay where they sit. His top half shoots out of the vehicle and lands on the median. And Vance lies broken, curses at the sky, inhales foul gusts of motor oil before that smell is overwhelmed by the blood in his throat, a sensation of drowning, then death.

One glance down tells Ludwig all he needs to know: his buddies, his homies, his brothers, are gone. Ludwig, inclined since youth to morbidity and a certain fatalism, thinks *so this is how it's gotta be*. Because he's thought about a lot of ways to die over his twenty-eight years, and especially the last two. But rocketing into the sky from the blown-out wreckage of a Humvee has never crossed his mind. Sure he's thought about getting *blown up*, but blown *up*? This way . . . this particular . . . *this* was never an option.

And so, above that modern highway in that ancient land that he neither knew much about nor cared much about nine months before that moment, and which he wouldn't have chosen to visit if he *had* known a thing or two about it, Ludwig comes to the apex of his flight, the breach of his rebirth as it were.

Spread-eagled, facing west, Ludwig spies quicksilver plumes of smoke rise into the morning sky above Fallujah. Then, spinning, he's overcome by the immensity of the stretch of sky in which he finds himself and is surprised to discover centered within it, as if deliberately to draw his attention, the sun, which isn't gold or yellow, or white or silver as all past experience would lead him to expect, but black, and densely so, a huge unblinking pupil surrounded by an azure-tinted iris. Ludwig blinks, freezes. And then he lunges at it. But his fingers don't feel a thing. He finds that this . . . black sun is still too far away. Because he'd hoped to find a purchase there, some way of holding on, his panic surges, and our hero, our fool, Ludwig Mason comes tumbling down.

Lucky for him, the force of the explosion has blasted him not just up but also out, away from the twisted and blazing wreckage. By the time he crashes to the blacktop highway, all his clothes have turned to cinder and half his hair has been singed to ash. He is a different man, remade, or better put, ready to be made. For he *is* new. His past is past. He is the stork's burnt offering.

1.

He wakes and hears a woman's voice list what ails him: a hematoma around his left clavicle, contusions on both thighs, first-degree burns on his calves and lower back. Her voice floats in clear on his left side but he doesn't hear anything through his right ear. The fact that he survived is a *miracle*, she says.

Charlotte, thinks Ludwig. *Sam.*

He wakes again. The air shudders and drones around him. Have minutes passed? Or hours? It's dark. He's lying on a pallet. He guesses he's in a vehicle, some kind of truck. He turns to his left, his right, sees others like him laid out in a row, red lights, and the silhouettes of marines seated with their backs against a wall. A skein of bright red webbing hangs above them.

He's on a transport plane.

"Someone's trying hard to reach you."

A nurse with a vaguely familiar vibe about her glances at something beside her. Ludwig turns to see. Phone messages lie scattered on the table beside his bed, messages from Charlotte set there for him, up to three a day some days. He's been in for nearly a week but he doesn't know what to do with them. In the days before that day in Fallujah he wanted nothing more than to talk with her, to hear her voice, but now—What the hell is he supposed to do with them? And if he does call her, when he can call her, what the fuck is he supposed to *say*?

He lies on his side as the nurse checks the bandages on his back.

"You're from Philly," she says.

"How'd you know?"

"Says so, on your chart."

"Huh."

"You got kids?"

"A boy." He blinks and sighs, exhausted. "A little boy." The faces of Wonder and Ferrer and Vance crowd his thoughts. Their laughter. The way they had made him laugh and everything he felt for them. He cannot comprehend—

"Stay with me now, Ludwig. Stay with me," she says. "I'm Sonia, okay? I'm here to help you. What's his name?"

"Who?"

"Your boy. Your son."

"Sam," he gasps. "Oh God. Sam." Overwhelmed with emotion, he weeps.

"Aw, c'mon now." She strokes his face and smiles. "I bet he's cute."

"Ah."

She traces her finger along his spine. "It's getting there." She pokes something raw and he winces.

"Feels fucking awful," he murmurs.

"Well, it's healing." She helps him roll onto his back.

"How much longer?" He wipes away the tears. "When can I go home?"

"I don't know. It's a mess. Lotsa people flying in. A lot of bad injuries."

Something about her holds his gaze until he feels his hand tremble on the bed rail. He stares at it. Does it really belong to him? He feels like he might throw up. She places her hand on his.

"You'll be okay. You know that, right?"

He sighs and looks about. "Doesn't feel like it," he whispers. The world feels jagged and undependable. Nothing seems right. His mind is filled with tiny black and white blooms, like fireworks. His face feels riddled by ticks and spasms. *Where are their bodies now*, he wonders. *Have they been buried?*

"You're alive. You made it."

"Not so sure."

"I'm guessing your son's counting on it."

"Can't imagine—I'd be useful to him."

She leans over the bed rail, touches his face. He wonders what it is about her.

"You're gonna make it, okay?" she says. "Just—keep at it."

———————

The guy they room him with at Landstuhl is another brother named Jason, who's from Houston. Jason lost an eye and got both arms crushed by a blown-in wall during fighting on the west side of the city. He lies in an induced coma. For the first few days they put Jason on oxycodone, but it doesn't work as well as they hoped, so they switch him to morphine, developments that Ludwig follows with a jittery, almost vampiric intensity.

Ludwig sleeps, he tries to sleep, he pretends to sleep. He stares at Jason's IV bag and listens to it *drip drip drip* until he wants to rip his good left ear off, since they'll only give him codeine.

A few days in, the dose of codeine they have him on isn't enough anymore. He jags for more. He craves the big doses of good stuff that got him through Baghdad, through Sadr City and Tikrit and those last days. And now, surrounded by dark, he hears his molars scrape against one another, a tectonic surge sweeps through him, leaving him feeling helpless and terrified. He clenches his fists around both rails and braces himself as he heads into the turbulence, the terrors, the shakes.

As soon as he can walk, he cases the place: each floor, every department, the nurses' stations, the stairwells, the exits and restrooms, kitchens and break rooms, custodial closets and storerooms.

When he doesn't feel up for walking, he reads or tries to read paperbacks cadged from the unit library—Walter Mosley, Tom Clancy, a weird, short history of the Knights Templar. Or he stares out the window in a state of utter stupefaction, eyes the sprawl of hospital buildings, access roads, and parking lots, the distant planes, small as toys, that arc across the sky toward Ramstein.

He kneels and squints at the dead-bolt Schlage under the doorknob. He sets at it with the screwdriver and the ball-peen hammer stolen that morning from an open utility closet. He jams it, wrenches at the base, manages to pry away a wedge of the laminate surrounding. Two minutes later he's in.

He shuts the door behind him, leans back against it in the dark, takes a deep breath. He feels for the light, turns it on, and finds himself at one end of a long aisle lined on both sides with shelves stacked deep with what looks like a mother lode. He edges forward, spots acne cream, antibiotics, and antihistamines, allergy drugs, aspirin, laxatives, and PMS pills. But as he studies the labels he grows desperate. Where's the Biphetamine? Where are the Ephedra and the Dexedrine? The Actiq and Vicodin? Where the fuck is the Duragesic? He can't even find Robitussin A-C or Tylenol with codeine.

At the end of the aisle he stops at a steel strong-room door with a dual-control combination lock. *Shit*, he whispers. He's never dealt with anything like this. His is a résumé of petty theft, of crimes of opportunity through street-level windows and alleyway doors, against small-time locks and junkers no one would miss, hot-wired and boosted off West Philly streets. He stares at it, overwhelmed by vertigo and desperation. Finally he pads back down the aisle. He turns off the light, slinks back into the dispensary office, waits, listens. When he thinks it's clear, he opens the door and steps into the hall. He hears a sound. He turns and spots her, Sonia, just turning the corner. She's carrying a brown paper bag and a bottle of orange juice. He steps between her and the damage he's done. She stops short and smiles when she sees him.

"Hey, what're you doing up?" she says.

"Ah, nothing. Just—can't sleep."

Her glance flits over his shoulder toward the closed door behind him. "You should rest."

"I will." He nods. "Just couldn't—sleep."

She heads on and he watches her turn the corner, but he catches her last, wary glance back before she vanishes.

Back in his room he washes his face, then stares at himself in the mirror. Jason snores in his dead sleep. Ludwig peers into his own dead eyes. *Fuck*, he whispers.

The dream is like a Greatest Hits reel. It repeats and repeats and repeats so that he is able to see everything that happened as if it were being replayed just for him. He gets to see it all play out from every angle:

He was blown into the sky by the force of two improvised explosive devices detonating against the side of the vehicle on which he was perched. So far as he can recall, Wonder must have seen or sensed the first IED before it blew, because he slowed the vehicle, giving Vance just enough time to yell "HEY! HEY! STOP! GET THE FUCK—" Before the expected, certain OUT became just that, the Humvee turned inside— like a violent lesson in cognition or linguistics: the thing itself preceding the name of the thing with such alchemical force that Ludwig felt as if he'd turned into fire.

The detonation of the first IED and the nearly simultaneous detonation of a second even more powerful IED ripped apart the Humvee's frame, cracked both axles, blew both front doors off, and turned the vehicle into a ball of fire. And that was that. Ludwig, standing in the gun turret behind the .50 cal had simply blown . . . up.

When he wakes, he suffers through the nights, the enveloping dark, the long hours filled with tremors and whispers and Jason's comatose snoring. *Can't they shut that fucker up?* he thinks. He decides he'll do it with a pillow, hold it firm over Jason's face until he stops his struggle. But first he puts his own pillow over his own head and tries to smother out the world. It works for a little while, like a crude isolation tank. But the darkness turns inside out and so do his thoughts, until he hears a spectral *Why you? Why yoou? Whyyyyy yoooou?* rise inside his head. It's a chant, some kind of taunt or threat sung by a dead-eyed chorus of three: Wonder and Ferrer and Vance, echoing, drowning out all his thoughts and even the sound of his teeth grating against one another. They're angry and they're coming to get him. They see no reason why he made it out and they didn't.

The menace, the threat, feels so immediate that he rolls out of bed and cowers under the window. At first he can hold on, but terror overwhelms him and he starts to scream. Two men run in and wrestle him into his bed but he can't—won't—stop. Why are they holding *him* down? he wonders. He loves his brothers, but they are dead. Their corpses, animated by rage, are scrabbling down the hall at that very moment. They'll burst into the room any second now.

"Ludwig."

Someone grips his chin. Eyes—a woman's—one of the doctors, stare into his.

"You're gonna be all right. Just take it easy now. Okay? We're gonna take care of you."

He can't find the words. He's hyperventilating. He feels like his lungs are filled with glue.

"Breathe."

He breathes. Sonia, who had reassured him only a few days before that everything would be all right, stands near the foot of the bed. He looks at the doctor.

"Help me," he whispers. "Help."

Her eyes soften. "How can we help? What kind of help do you need, Ludwig?"

He gestures for her to lean closer. "You—you guys got anything for like—like staying awake?"

She squints at him. "You mean something to help you sleep?"

"No, no. To *stay* awake. Go pills? Dex? Modafinil? Any—anything like that?"

Her smile tightens. Her eyes narrow. "You really need to rest. Why don't you just rest now? Okay? I'll have someone stay nearby, if you need someone."

"Just—please. Anything."

Her eyes flatten. "I'll have to think about that," she says. It's like she's seen through him or like she's seen him many times before and lost interest.

"Anything. Please. Anything."

They turn the lights out and leave. He listens to Jason snore, watches the light through the blinder slats above Jason's bed, the light that washes the hallway floor in a gauzy green glow. He closes his eyes.

He isn't going to make it. He knows it. The thing inside of him that has served for all of his life until now as a kind of floor or platform on which to stand has caved in. He'd taken it for granted and now it's gone. He came out of that day in Fallujah almost unscathed, at least physically, but now he knows, he understands that the bottom of his head or brain, his soul or whatever the hell it is, has been sheared off or blown off like a limb. He needs to hang on to the inside of his head and see how long he'll last, but he doesn't feel confident. He'll lose his strength, he'll lose his grip, and then he'll tumble and this time he won't land. His lungs narrow again and he gulps for air. His teeth chatter.

"Ludwig? Ludwig?"

He opens his eyes. Light shines through the blinds. It's that nurse. Sonia. She's with one of the men who held him down earlier. But when was that? Is it morning already? It seems they left just— He remembers noises, an alarm out in the hallway. *Oh God*, he thinks. He's losing it. He's lost it. She grips his arm with gloved hands and taps at it. She holds up a syringe, lances the cap of an upturned bottle.

"What's that?"

"Provigil. Modafinil. It'll help you ease back into things."

The shot in his arm, when it comes, is such a welcome relief, he laughs out loud.

"Thank you," he whispers. "Thank you. Thank you."

She presses a wad of gauze and tape into the crook of his arm. "No problem, buddy. Just rest. Just close your eyes and rest."

What's strange to him is how calm it makes him feel. In Fallujah, in the other places, in the middle of all that craziness, the stuff had hopped him up, made him feel like he could go for days. Back there, back then, it had made him feel like the bullets from the .50 cal were streaming out of his dick. Ludwig wants to hug her, to thank her, to say how much this means to him, but she's shrinking, vanishing along with the man beside her, the open doorway behind them, the entire room, the hospital, the world.

———

Sonia wears a strange pendant around her neck, a tiny cross with a loop at its top, or maybe it's a key? He looks at her. Although he continues to believe he knows her from somewhere, or that she bears an uncanny resemblance to someone he knows, she also seems completely out of place. Her face is delicate, refined. Her big, almond-shaped eyes draw him in, and she keeps her hair, a rich black mass, tightly bound in an army-standard bun. What is it about her, he wonders? What is she? And where does she come from? Is she Ethiopian? Somalian? Egyptian? Is she half of one thing and something else? And the way she looks at him—does she feel it too? A strange familiarity?

He sips water from a paper Dixie cup with his unclaimed hand. Why can't he keep his arm from shaking? "I feel like I know you," he confesses.

She smiles as she presses the plunger of the syringe. The heat radiates from his shoulder to his forearm and his neck. Ludwig closes his eyes. There is a little rush of vertigo on the runway to calm.

"You do," she says. "In a way."

"I don't—follow you." His own voice sounds like it's coming from the end of a tunnel.

"You went to Kelpius High School, right? Back in Philly?"

He opens his eyes. The unexpected sound of his school's name, out of context, warps the air and turns things fuzzy. "Yeah, that's right. How—" His throat catches. The heat has overtaken his chest. He swallows. "How do you know? My—my file?"

She sets aside the spent syringe and presses the gauze into the crook of his arm. When she lets go he holds his palm over the cotton, blinks, waiting for the calm, eager to stop thinking.

"I'm from Jersey—Camden. But I used to live in Overbrook when I was a kid. I went to junior high there. I know your hood."

He'd hoped that with clarity the fuzziness would straighten out. But the mention of Kelpius and Overbrook blurs things even more. He suspects she's given him a tainted batch.

"Overbrook? Jesus—that's like, right around the corner."

She smiles. He grins but he's feeling loopy. He feels the heat in his spine and his belly now. He's fading, convinced he's in a dream, some kind of hallucination. His eyes settle on the strange pendant.

"What?" she says, her smile turning to a quizzical frown.

"This—" He reaches toward her and touches it.

"Ah," she says, setting her fingers over his. "This is the ankh."

She takes his hand and holds it. His body is now suffused by the heat. Each breath, each inhalation, draws into his body a hint of the joyful essence of life, of the way things *could be*, if only—if only— He closes his eyes.

"What is it?" he murmurs. "What does it mean?"

"Mmh," he hears her say. "I don't know if it's worth explaining right now. You're fading fast. You're falling asleep."

And he is, and he does.

———

He leans over, pulls open the drawer of the credenza beside his bed, and reaches in for the deck of water-stained photos salvaged from his gear. He stares at the photos depicting the boy, the beautiful woman, the man—him—with them, grinning, happy as can be it seems.

———

One morning—it could be the next, or maybe days have passed—he wakes and finds Sonia standing over him.

"I know you," he says.

She doesn't smile. "In a way, I guess you do."

His mouth feels like it's filled with sand. She draws the blinds and he winces. His Cyclops roommate Jason is gone. The bed is empty, the sheets look as flat and inert as if no man had ever lain there. Ludwig wonders what Jason's voice sounds like. It was as if he'd never been, as if the intensity of his trauma had recreated or transformed him, but also negated him, despite the fact that he'd survived. Ludwig opens his own eyes again.

"Hey, listen, Ludwig," she says. "Talking about home. We're getting all these messages at the nurses' station. You really need to call your family."

He turns his gaze to the window across the room, blinks. "I— I will."

———————

Evening, dinnertime. He sits at one of the computer stations in the library staring at the subject line of an email from Charlotte that says *Please call*. The body reads *now*. What fixates him are the letters in her message that spell a moment in time, *n-o-w*, a moment that once considered—once you might think you had hold of—would already have escaped.

The marine down the way coughs, and Ludwig jolts out of his trance. He looks around. The library is a cocoon of hushed silence. A group of people seated in a meeting room behind a glass wall watches Sonia, who is standing at a whiteboard. All of the writing on the board is in Spanish, he sees. He watches her. She glimpses him over the heads of her audience and smiles. He smiles back and turns back to the computer.

What to say? What to say? he thinks. He stares at the screen, sighs, clicks reply, and types, *I'll call. Just need some time.* He stares at that last word for a moment before he clicks send.

———————

He sits with Sonia over coffee in the therapy center break room.

"How'd you get into all this?" he asks.

"All what?"

"Army. Germany."

She shrugs. "When my ex and I split up, I was on my own with my daughter, and I—"

"You've got a kid?"

Her eyes narrow a little. "Yeah."

He watches her: her strong jaw, her eyes—brown—edged by a hazel halo like a highlight.

"What's her name?"

"Rania."

"How old is she?"

"She's twelve." She hesitates, cracks a smile. "Twelve going on thirty."

"Huh. Cool."

"I didn't have a lot going before that. I worked at a restaurant in Camden, waitressing, but we were barely making it. Realized I needed something—wanted something I could hold on to so we'd be okay. So I decided on nursing, but I needed money for school. Army seemed like the way to go."

"Huh. That's great." Ludwig grins. She's been extraordinarily kind to him. But in that moment he's overtaken by a sadistic impulse. After hearing her story, he feels no patience for the terrible choices of others. He's still reckoning with his own. "I bet you've got no regrets."

Her smile twitches, shuts down. He can tell that she can't tell where he's coming from, and that makes him smile even more.

"That's—not funny," she says, frowning.

As soon as she says it he regrets what he's done. He sits back, quirks his lip, and mulls an apology, but his mind is not his own. He taps his disembodied fingers against the table, averts his gaze. Beyond the window snow swirls in a mesmerizing static under the lot lights. He scans the memos and photos and magnets that cover the refrigerator door behind her, registers the buzz of the fluorescent bulbs above their heads and the hum of the microwave on the shelf behind him. Every surface radiates: heat, light, an infant-like hum; all of it buzzes. He turns to her again. She sits leaning forward so close, too close. He looks at her as much to center himself as to start to try to make amends.

"Looking forward to Christmas?" he says.

"Sure," she says, but it isn't in her eyes. Her eyes are on him and they're wary.

"I'm sorry," he says. He shakes his head. "I don't know why I said that."

Time bends and warps around her gaze until he senses that there's more to it, a communication similar to the buzzing all around him, but different, human, warm. She reaches across and strokes his cheek with her thumb. At first her eyes don't give a thing, but her lips bow in a mournful smile. She places her hand on his and holds it. It's as if she's having the same dream, or nightmare, or whatever this is. He knows they're not supposed to fraternize, but he wonders what difference it can make. What brig can be bleaker than the inside of his head? He's busted up. His mind is lost somewhere, misplaced like a hat—or a key.

2.

She tells him that she has an apartment in town, in Landstuhl. She tells him that she thinks it might do him some good to leave the hospital, come over, share some time away from prying eyes. So she finds him boots that look brand-new, fresh fatigues, and a good thick coat, and one night, toward the start of his third week in, after she gives him his shot, she busts him out.

He's surprised to see that she drives a BMW. It's black, a compact model he's never seen in the States, but even so, the casual luxury of it throws him off.

"It's a friend's," she says cryptically, as if reading his mind. She pulls it into gear, curves along the access road and out the exit to the highway.

It hits Ludwig that he's in Germany. He hasn't yet internalized this or girded himself for the world *outside* the hospital, a world that he's come to believe he'll never know again. Everything feels unfamiliar. He takes solace when Sonia lifts her grip briefly from the knob to squeeze his knee. She drives fast, but all the cars are moving fast. Lucky for him, the modafinil slows things down, a paradoxical outcome of long-term use in the Box. In the shadows, in the fast-moving car, he watches the oncoming headlights blur into phosphorous streaks.

She parks in the lot of a complex of three-story beige-brick apartments. As they walk up a path he starts to lose his nerve again, but the smile she flashes as she unlocks the door renews his resolve. He follows her down a hallway to a living room where a girl with long black hair, who looks Arab, dressed in a green T-shirt and jean skirt, slow-dances to Cypress Hill:

> *I want to get high, so high.*
> *I want to get high, so high.*
> *Well, that's the funk*
> *Elastic, the blunt I twist it.*
> *The slamafied (buddafied) funk on*
> *Your discus . . .*

The dancing girl's eyes are shut. A man with slicked-back, sandy-blond hair sits on a sofa beyond her, hunched over a table littered with wine and beer bottles, glasses, overflowing ashtrays, and a mess of CD jewel cases. He lights a cigarette with a silver Zippo and squints up from reading liner notes.

"Allo, baby," he says.

"Hey," says Sonia.

But she doesn't stop and she doesn't introduce the man. Ludwig follows her past a kitchen and down another hall to an unlit room. When she turns on the light, he's startled to find that every surface—the floor, the walls, the ceiling—is painted in concentric bands or circles, each of a different color: a black dot in the middle of the floor, half obscured by the edge of a bed, radiates to red, to brown, orange, shades of yellow and continues upward to contract again in a gold dot surrounding the baseplate of the light fixture in the center of the ceiling.

"Whoa," he says.

"I wanted it to be like the inside of the sun," she says as she sets her keys down on the nightstand.

She crosses the room and rummages over a desk strewn with CDs, magazines, a small boom box. She puts a CD in, hovers over the player. Lauryn Hill's *Miseducation* starts to play, one of those parts between the songs. Sounds are clearer now, through Ludwig's right ear. A teacher asks *Whattayou think about love?* The kids laugh. *Break it down*, the teacher says. *Break it down*. A boy shouts, *Love is just a feeling.*

Ludwig watches Sonia light four thick yellow candles set on small plates on the dresser. Beside them stands a half-full bottle of Jack Daniel's. She twists the cap off, takes a swig. Ludwig steps toward the rows of photos taped to the wall above the desk. They're pictures of little kids, boys and girls. All sit in hospital beds, all are injured in some way or other—a bandaged head here, a burnt shoulder there, a boy whose legs are missing below the knees. There are about twenty of them and all of them are smiling at the camera.

"Where is this?" he says.

"Green Zone." She stands beside him and hands him the bottle. "Eighty-Sixth Combat Support."

He swallows a mouthful of whiskey, blinks hard at a picture of a little boy whose arms stop at the elbows. He wants to look away but finds he can't. "These are"—his throat catches—"really sad."

"The whole thing is," she murmurs as she steps away.

He stares at the picture, touches the edge of the boy's face, mesmerized by the brightness of his eyes. How much older than Sam might that boy be? "After my dad died," he says, "me and my mom found a box of his stuff. It had some pictures in it, kinda like these. Pictures of my dad from when he was in Nam, pictures of people he knew there, and there were some pictures of kids he must've known, in cities, in villages."

"What did he do?" asks Sonia. "Like, for a living?"

"He was a teacher, a music teacher. But he was sick a lot."

"Sick? What with?"

When Ludwig turns, he finds Sonia sitting at the edge of the bed, leaned forward, elbows on knees, watching him. "Don't really know. He went to Nam when he was young. He was like nineteen. Marines. He must've seen a lot of crazy shit. He never talked about it, though. My mom used to say he never really came home. At least, not all of him."

"I'm sorry to hear that," she says. She stares at him.

"It's okay." He hesitates, but not for long. He goes to her and kisses her. She pulls the bottle from his hand, takes another pull, and sets it on the nightstand. She passes her hands over his chest and lies back. He reaches down and strokes her face, her neck, the inside of her thigh through her camouflage pants. How slender she is. How soft the kiss had felt. But he wonders if this is right. Maybe Sonia senses his doubt. She sits up. Her eyes follow her hands as they unfasten his buckle and pull at his pants. She kisses his abdomen, his hip. He's drawn toward it, the place they're surely headed, but his eyes snag on the photographs above the desk, and he wants her to stop. He thinks of taking her hand and stopping her, but he takes the bottle and drinks instead. Maybe she's used to this? Screwing under pictures of these kids burned and blown apart? Maybe the pictures explain why she moves as if in a dream, why her movements feel languorous, so tinged with a resignation and sadness that pulls him like a tidal force? Or maybe he just imagines that her thoughts, her feelings mirror his own? Maybe *he*'s the one leading them further into this strange space between them?

He closes his eyes and turns to shut out the kids. He doesn't want to look again. When he opens his eyes, he notices in the corner to his right, beside the closet door, a waist-high shrine of some sort, very ornate, with three drums, each of different size, wood carvings, a slender stringed instrument, sticks of incense in little brass bowls, framed pictures of people—an old woman, a young man holding a laughing girl aloft—painted pictures the size of index cards, of animals that look as if from myths, or maybe they are gods?

"What's that?" he says.

She glances over her shoulder and smiles. "That's my world," she says. "That's my mojo."

He understands that although he knows a few things about Sonia—the fact that she spent some part of her childhood in Philly, the fact that she has a daughter, a few things here and there, fragments of affinity that form a comforting albeit narrow perch in a reality where nothing much feels real—he doesn't *really* know her. She remains a mystery to him. He would like to have more time to talk, to forget the pictures of the kids, or at least find out more about them, to *lead into* things and learn more, to ask her just what she means by what she said, but she reaches into his shorts and—and does it really matter?

She lets her hair down and he runs his fingers through the cascade of black curls that form a spectacular halo around her face. He can't get enough of it. She whispers things into his ears that sound romantic and obscene in a mix of languages. He catches snippets of Spanish, of French, but others are a mystery to him. From her bold brown eyes, his gaze traces down to the black slit of her navel nestled at the center of an ornate tattoo, an oval with sinuous tendrils. Instinct, intuition—this impulsive intimacy—tell him that it is not the sun he knows but some far distant star. Ludwig breathes deep the smell of sweat and salt, a smell that makes him think of nights spent watching, waiting and watching, until a welcome peace falls, under the lull of Sonia's breathing.

Later, he stirs and wakes to find her astride him. Her neck, her shoulders, her breasts glow in the candlelight. She moves with great deliberation. Ludwig sighs. He runs his hands along her thighs, around her hips. She moves faster. He holds her tight as her thighs engulf him. She gasps toward the apex of the sun in the ceiling. He feels like he's tumbling into her, feels awash again in the sensation of falling up until she collapses beside him and falls asleep. He sleeps too.

When he wakes, he finds her entwined around him, her hand resting on his chest. He looks down and sees a black shape, a circle or an oval, smeared around her splayed fingers. He holds up her hand. What is it? Her fingers are covered with it. On the nightstand, beside the whiskey bottle, lies a brass bowl filled with black powder or grease that smells like some sweet spice, like cinnamon or nutmeg, but mixed with something sharp smelling. Sonia nuzzles his neck and murmurs. Ludwig retreats, rises, pulls on his pants, grabs his boots and other things.

Across the hall he finds the bathroom. He shuts the door and turns on the light. There, in the mirror, he sees it, a shape on his chest that looks like a crude copy of the symbol on her belly. He splashes water on it to wash it off. But it's oily, waxy, both. It smears and he can't get clean. Still drunk, he fumbles as he strips and climbs into the shower, washes his chest, his face, his body with soap and hot water. After, he dries himself with a hand towel and confirms that he is free of the symbol.

He pulls on his pants and shirt. He's shocked to glimpse in the fog-coated mirror the face of the same man who stares back at him from the photos of his family. That man is the last person he wants to see, so he opens the cabinet, scans the shelves, and spots a bottle of Tylenol, a bag of plastic razors, a can of shaving cream, toothpaste, a plastic cup filled with cotton swabs. There's nothing of interest. Nothing of use.

He shuts the cabinet door, rubs the condensation off the mirror, and freezes when he sees *the little girl in the backseat, the whites of her eyes dulled to taupe, still as a moldering doll, bloated in the summer heat. Flies, startled by the unexpected light, burst off her face. Ludwig turns. Wonder, standing at the top of the embankment, is watching him, his face a frown of worry.*

"What'd you see, man?" he calls. "What is it?"

"I don't know," Lud says. "Not sure." He takes a step back. Scratches his cheek. Wonder is a sensitive guy. If he gets wind that there's a kid in there, things will get emotional really fucking fast. "Call for backup," shouts Ludwig. "We might need to tow this thing outta here."

"All right, but be careful, man. Don't touch anything. Just take it easy."

Wonder turns away, says something into his radio, and soon more guys are sauntering up the road to see what's going on. The car is at an angle. The door isn't completely submerged. To satisfy his curiosity, and before the crowd gets too big, Ludwig yanks on the handle and pulls it open. The heat. The stench. He wretches and spits in the water and covers his nose and mouth, but he can't look away. He leans in, turns to his left. The windshield is riddled with bullet holes. A dead man sits crumpled forward onto the steering wheel. Ludwig peers forward. The girl is so small. And what is that in her hand? He leans in. The heat. He gasps. It's a strange card, like a playing card but different. He hears the men starting to climb down the embankment behind him, and he feels a terrible contempt for them all, especially for himself. Why rush? Really? He thinks. What's the fucking hurry? He curses and gasps and spits. What can they do for this little girl? He leans farther in. He's afraid to touch her but what the hell is—what's that card in her hand?

When he comes to, he finds the man there, staring back at him. But he understands now that it's *him*, the man he once knew. The man who can't exist because there can't be two of him now, now that he's different or changed or whatever it is that's happened. He punches the mirror. The blow makes a sickening thud. The panel bows in, in a circle. He pulls his hand away. Shards tinkle into the sink. A skein of cracks remains, dyed red by the blood flowing from three dime-size flaps of flesh on his knuckles. He grabs his coat, his boots and lunges out the door. In the hall he hesitates at the sight of Sonia's closed bedroom door—did she hear him?

When he reaches the living room, he finds the blond man hunched over a scattered deck of cards, doing sleight of hand like he's practicing a magic trick. Sam Cooke croons on the stereo. The girl twirls in slow circles in the dimly lit kitchen like a windup toy with a busted mainspring. The man looks up and rises.

"What— *Mein Gott*. What happened to you?"

Ludwig looks down. Blood from his hand drips to the rust-colored carpet. "Ah—shit. Sorry. Cut myself, on the mirror—an accident."

"I thought I had heard something—" The man darts down the hall. Ludwig watches him go into the bathroom, cross the hall, and enter Sonia's room. Ludwig hesitates. He feels like he should explain himself, but he doesn't want to go back down the hall. The man comes back.

"Is she awake?" asks Ludwig.

"She's passed out," the man says. "I woke her, briefly, and she said she was fine. Then she passed out." He frowns. "You didn't—hurt her, did you?"

Ludwig freezes, holds up his hands. "No. No way, man. I was just—I, I cut my hand on the mirror in there."

The man nods with a shadow of skepticism. His gaze settles on Ludwig's hand. "You should clean that," he says. "Like, now. Here—" He brushes past the girl, into the kitchen. "Let me see if I can find something." He pulls cabinet doors and drawers open. "Maybe there are plasters."

"Plasters?"

"Bandages. Bandages."

Finally he abandons the search, hands Ludwig a wad of paper towels torn from a roll on the counter. Ludwig presses it to his knuckles. The guy looks genuinely concerned.

"*Ach.* Is there glass? Ay-yai-yai, terrible." He shakes his head. "Terrible. Listen, man. Listen. I'm Otto. Whatever you need." He sounds like a German who's spent a lot of time in the US. "How can I help you?"

"I need a ride back."

"A ride? Mmmh. I can give you a ride. No problem. What's your name?"

"Ludwig."

"*Ludwig?* Ha! That's a *German* name!" He grins and turns to the dancing girl, but she doesn't open her eyes. He looks at Ludwig and shrugs. "So we go?"

In Sonia's car, or maybe Otto's, heading back to Landstuhl, Ludwig tries to focus on the road ahead. He's feeling dazed, a little nauseated, not in a talkative mood. But Otto keeps turning from the wheel to glance at him. Ludwig knows that as much as he wants it to, the silence can't last. It never does. Finally:

"Man. What happened back there? Did Sonia see what happened? Did she see it?"

"No." Ludwig hesitates. Then, to change the subject and because he wants to know, he says, "How do you two know each other?"

"Ah. We are—friends."

"Huh."

"Don't get me wrong," says Otto. "Things—Well, there's nothing between us."

"But there was?"

"Well, maybe. It's hard to tell. There was a time of some craziness."

"What kinda craziness was that?"

"Ach. I don't know. Confused, self-destructive craziness." Otto glances at Ludwig's hand cradled in his lap. "I guess you could say, the kind of thing that can lead a man to put his fist in a mirror."

Ludwig looks at the sentry row of streetlights along the side of the road ahead. "This has got nothing to do with her," he says.

They travel in silence until Ludwig asks Otto to stop just before the access road leading up to the hospital. Ludwig climbs out and shuts the door. Gusts of his breath cloud the frigid night air. The passenger-side window retracts.

"They'll let you in?" says Otto.

"I hope so. Thanks for the ride."

"No problem. Okay. Good luck, brother." Otto puts the car into drive and flashes a V. "Peace."

Ludwig watches Otto drive away. Later, after getting grilled for half an hour by three MPs and finally convincing them that he got locked out after cadging a cigarette for a smoke in the parking lot, they let him into the hospital.

Back in his room, he goes to the bathroom, shuts the door, and peels away the bloody clump of paper towels. A cracked crust of dried blood and paper fibers have congealed to his broken skin. He washes his hand and watches the blood run down the drain. He sees that the man in the mirror is himself, a man he understands in the aftermath of the night's long and disorienting buzz is some kind of combination of who he was and what he is. The problem he faces is that there is a gap between, but he's too tired to gauge how wide that gap is. He lies down in his bed and struggles to figure out if what happened really *did* happen until he falls asleep.

The next day he sticks as close to his room as he can to avoid Sonia. But she never shows. Finally late in the afternoon of the following day, he goes looking for her. But he finds no trace of her. When he asks around, he finds out that she's flown stateside. She got rotation orders to Walter Reed Medical Center in DC and flew out from Ramstein the night before.

3.

Early December, aught four. He's been in for more than three weeks when they ship him back still tender but better off, at least physically, as a Christmas gift he's too numb to appreciate. All the way home people thank Ludwig for his service to the country: the hospital staff with a party for about 150 men and women with music and balloons and cake and streamers and everything, the flight crew on the trip back stateside, the base commander at Camp Pendleton, who pins the Purple Heart and the Marine Corps Expeditionary Medal on his chest on a wet and windy day.

Later, studying the medals, Ludwig realizes he'll be the only one who'll remember how Vance, below, had yelled *Hey! Hey! What the——?* as they sped toward the pile of suspicious-looking concrete on the side of the road. But that was over. That was past. Ludwig understands that no one needs to know anything more about it.

After a red-eye to Philadelphia, he catches a train headed north. Snow tumbles on the city of his birth. His mother died only a couple years ago. His father died long ago. There's an older half brother out there, his father's other son, somewhere in the suburbs far west. But, despite all the effort his father had put into trying to forge a bond between them, their relationship had never taken hold. The last time Ludwig saw his brother was when they both stood over their father's grave.

At 30th Street Station, he takes a bus west and another one north into the patchwork of neighborhoods that for most of his life were all he knew but which he now barely recognizes. When he knocks at his own front door, Charlotte opens it. She's clutching Sam. She stares at him with an expression of rage mixed with the wound he's inflicted by his absence and by his prolonged silence. Then she grabs him tight. Her face is as wounded and regal as he remembers, an upside-down teardrop, a portrait of timid arrogance.

"Oh God," she cries and moans. "Oh, Ludwig. Oh my God."

Sam clings to her neck. How old is the boy now? he wonders. Two and a half? He'd been less than a few months old when Ludwig had first left for the Box. Ludwig holds up a small stuffed bear dressed in Marine fatigues. Sam blinks, but the eye that isn't pressed against his mother's shoulder stares back at Ludwig with startling intensity. It's filled with fear, expectation, a mix of emotions so dense and inscrutable that Ludwig squints for any hint of recognition, any spark of the familiar.

Charlotte hugs Ludwig tight again. He's amazed at how strong she is. He holds her close in turn because he imagines that that's what the man he's supposed to be would do. She pulls back and looks him up and down. She sees his bandaged fist. "Oh God. Your hand."

He touches it and covers the bandage. He nearly forgot. She reaches for it, hesitates, and grips his shoulder instead.

"Is that—is that what happened?"

Ludwig nods. What can he tell her? What can he say? There'd been stretches of days and weeks so fucked up over there, stretches when he'd been so afraid for his life or the lives of his guys that he'd barely thought of her and Sam. Or, perversely, he'd thought of them with a kind of obsessive fixation that doesn't jibe with the reality of their solid bodies now encircled by his arms. Does he even have those kinds of words? He doubts it. So he keeps his mouth shut and tries hard to believe that this isn't a dream. He tries hard to believe that he's home.

4.

Ludwig sits on the western embankment of Fairmount Park and watches gulls fly over the water. He studies the shimmering surface of the Schuylkill River, the farther bank across the way. He envisions the encampments, the settlements and villages, the relentless encroachment of new settlers on the original inhabitants, the whole thing metastasizing, congealing, growing into the city, and he wonders if all this, too, had once been an untamed wilderness? A primal place, full of chaos and violence as he has come to believe all places are at their cores, below their surfaces? *It must have been*, he thinks. *It must have.* He rises from his perch and sets off, homeward bound, except for one, impulsive detour.

Blocks away, on Poplar, he knocks at the door of a narrow red row house. No one answers, so he bends at the window and peers past the angled blind slats. He spies a tidy living room, a low shelf lined with toys, a hallway leading to a kitchen, an infant's high chair set beside a table. As he walks back toward the corner he bumps into her. Shelly's carrying a bag of groceries, and she's wearing her blue-and-yellow SaveRight vest.

"Hey," she says. She hands him the groceries as if he's shown up just in time for that very purpose, lights a cigarette, and takes a long drag. "Whattup?"

"Nothin' much."

"You stalkin' me?"

"Naw." He smiles. "Just sayin' hi. How's Oscar? How's your aunt?"

"They're good," she says. She presses her forefinger hard against his chest. "Why you all dressed up? You gotta job?"

"No. I had an interview."

"Oh yeah?" Shelly grins. "How'd it go?"

"It went."

"Ouch." She winces, takes a drag on her cigarette. "You know, if you go in and talk to those assholes and beg a little, I bet they'd take you back. It was just—"

"It's all right."

"It wasn't fair they kept me. We shouldn't have been fucking around like that—"

"Shh. Shh. It's no big deal, baby. Let it go."

He smiles at Shelly. She pushes her hair out of her eyes. She smells sweet, even at the end of the day. She has always stood out, just as Charlotte has always stood out. The fact that Charlotte and Shelly's friendship, forged in high school, has curdled and collapsed is not entirely his fault. There had always been a rivalry, like a high-voltage rail between them. His mistake has been in lying across it both figuratively and literally. He lives in fear that Charlotte will discover this. But Shelly's smoky voice, the black denim and the blue shirt and blue-and-yellow vest of her uniform entice him from good caution, remind him of illicit moments that past spring in the SaveRight stockroom, before he and Shelly got careless, before they got caught.

"What're you up to?" she says. "Why're you lookin' at me like that?"

"I'm just— Just been— Thought maybe you might wanna, you know, hang out."

"Hang out."

"Yeah," he says.

She peers at him over her sunglasses with sloe, catlike eyes.

"Hey," he says. "Only if you—"

She shifts, takes another drag. "Listen, Lud, Jimmy's my man, you know that, right?"

"Yeah, baby, of course I know. I—"

"Don't baby me. Listen to me. Listen. Problem is, Jimmy likes to hang out too. Once a month Jimmy likes to come home from wherever the hell he's been, to play with his *fucking son* for fifteen minutes."

"Hey, hey, it's—"

"Then he wants to fuck me."

Ludwig cringes. Jimmy is a trucker, a brother five or six years older than both of them. He is, Ludwig understands, a bit crazy, prone to conspiracy thinking and unpredictable mood swings complicated by years of substance abuse. Shelly has mentioned a couple times that Jimmy owns a handgun.

"Then he *fucks himself* up. Beer, whiskey, pot, coke, meth—anything he can get his hands on. Then he *cries* and he *sobs* and he *promises* he'll get his shit straight this time around. And then he *vanishes*." She snaps her fingers. "Just like that, for days on end." She squints at him cockeyed. "Is that the kinda hangin' out you're talkin' about?"

"Jesus. Shelly. Fuck. What the—"

"Listen. What you and me had"—she touches his face—"was no small thing. But I don't wanna *hang out* anymore. I've got Oscar and he's all I've got and I've gotta protect him. His fucking father sure as hell won't." She takes another long drag on her cigarette and flicks it into the street. "Maybe he just can't," she says absently, with a sigh, before turning her attention back to him.

"Lud, bud, you got a kid, too, a wife, a fucking *family*. Weird to say, but I really wish I could hang with Charlotte again, like back in the day. I was just thinking that the other day, that I've got more in common with her than anybody else in this goddamn town." She gazes up the street. "I never woulda thought those might've been the best days." She turns and blinks at him, as if waking from her own dream. "So how'bout you go home now." She takes the bag of groceries, kisses his cheek. "Shoo. Get outta here. Go hang out with your family."

She heads off. A quarter block down she stops in front of her house and waves the back of her hand at him. "Scoot!" she shouts before climbing the stairs and vanishing into the house.

———————

Later, at home, he watches Charlotte shuttle cardboard boxes from the bedroom closet to the dining room table.

"I don't get it," she says. "Linda said you'd be perfect for it."

"I don't know, baby. The guy said some stuff about a cash-flow problem." The lie slips off his tongue. "Can't hire right now." Set loose in the room, he wonders how soon it will scramble back to bite him.

Earlier that month, Charlotte had discovered that the husband of one of the other receptionists at the law firm needed help with his business, something to do with data entry. So she'd looked into it and scheduled Ludwig for an interview, all before Ludwig could say no or think up a feasible stall. That morning, after Charlotte had taken Sam to her mother's and headed off to work, Ludwig had put on his khakis and his good white shirt and set out. But instead of going to the job interview, as he'd been expected to, he'd loitered briefly on Girard Avenue, trekked nearly three miles south and listened to tunes in a music store on Baltimore, had a slice of pie with coffee in a diner off Viola Street, and then meandered north to gaze at strangers, joggers, bicyclists, and other passersby in Fairmount Park before perching on the embankment of the Schuylkill to watch life and the river flow by.

Now it's evening and Charlotte's working on her thing, a kind of asymmetric war she's been fighting with the Marine Corps and the IRS since around the time Ludwig landed in the Box. It's all about a complicated mix of fuckups and snafus to do with health insurance and maternity and combat zone benefits, clerical errors on the garnishment of his wages, and some other stuff that had sounded really important when Ludwig was in the Box, outside of those bursts of terror when people were shooting at him.

In downtimes, while he was away, in letters and in emails, he'd expressed admiration for the way she fought the good fight. He had written that the only other place he'd seen that kind of ferocity and crazed determination was in men fighting hand to hand in the rubble of blasted-out buildings. And this was true. He had also said he would help her when he got back. But now, settling back into the "real world," or trying to, he understands that she's defending them against a clearer and more present danger than anything Saddam Hussein could've thrown at them. She's fighting for their survival. He understands, with great frustration and regret, that he's no better equipped to help her than she would have been equipped to help him during those battles in the Box. He also now understands that she can turn the withering anger and frustration that fuels her war on the US Department of Defense, the Internal Revenue Service, and the United

States Marine Corps on *him*, at any time, unexpectedly, and with the same passionate intensity.

Despite these cheerless insights, Ludwig feels that if he can figure out what it is that Charlotte wants—what word or act will give her peace or the security she needs—he'll gladly say or do it—

"This has to end," she says. "You have to get started on *something*. If we don't start making more money, we'll—"

—except for the part about getting a job *right* away. He sits on the couch, which is also now his bed, watching television, a reality show in which a pair of families have swapped each other's savage children for two whole weeks. He knows that this reality TV thing has really taken off since he went to Parris Island. People can't seem to get enough of the stuff. But he wonders whether it's legal for parents to give up their children that way, even if only temporarily. Aren't there labor laws or child welfare laws to stop people from doing stuff like that? Regardless, he hopes that if he keeps his eyes on the tube, if he doesn't make eye contact with Charlotte as she crosses back and forth in front of the television in that anxious, high-octane march of rage, that he might somehow become invisible to her. He might vanish and she will find herself promoting the material and psychological bene-fits of gainful employment to an empty room.

"—that's a hundred and twenty dollars," she continues. "But it's just for the day care. That doesn't even include the meal plan. And then my mom says—"

A plate of fried Vienna sausages, half eaten, lies on the table in front of him. Beside it lies a piece of paper covered with doodles of the black sun. The kids on the TV, two boys, start to tear apart the living room. Their temporary father stands helpless, shouts at them to stop. But the boys leap over the furniture like baboons high on a cocktail of crack and methamphetamine.

"—Ludwig? Ludwig, are you listening?" Charlotte steps in front of the TV. "I've got no intention of borrowing more money from my mom. You know we owe your aunt Jeanette over fifteen hundred dollars."

Ludwig, startled, cornered, tries to be useful. He shrugs. "Well at least your mom and my aunt won't charge us interest."

"What the—" She stops, glares at him confounded. "Are you—are you *here?* I'm not *fucking joking.* This isn't a fucking joke. You were gone forever and now you're barely here. There's *nothing* to show for it. We've got nothing," she shouts as she storms off.

Ludwig winces because she's right. He *is* barely there and he *was* gone a long, long time, even though time over there, in the Box, had often felt like it had stretched and contracted, stretched and contracted like a rubber band. But at moments like this between them, he finds it best to simply disengage, keep his head down, and lie low. And he does just that, just then. Ludwig sits, half-asleep on the couch, and watches as one of the children on the TV show shatters an heirloom clock against a dining room floor.

A little later he falls asleep splayed out on the couch and dreams a dream of bloody violence in which he chases down Charlotte and shatters her face with a fist so outsized it crushes her skull to a pulp.

Sam cries out and Ludwig wakes. Ludwig sees that Charlotte has abandoned the insurance forms and taxes. He sits until the terror boiling in his chest and guts cools down and his sweat-stained undershirt is dry. Finally the trauma of the dream, his curiosity, and his loneliness get the better of him. He pads down the hall, stands outside of Sam's room and listens: Charlotte shushes and coos. She sings Sam a song. Sam sings along as best he can. He giggles. They whisper endearments. Ludwig listens like a stranger, a beggar, an outcast. The spite he feels toward Charlotte is tempered by his dependency on her.

Toward the boy he feels a bald resentment. The warmth of their love radiates through the closed door, a heat he suspects might comfort his stricken heart. But he knows better than to go in there. He bites his lip till it bleeds.

Back in the kitchen, he listens and waits. He opens the pantry door and reaches for the topmost shelf. Behind a row of empty Tupperware containers and jars he finds the bottle of whiskey he keeps there for moments like this. He goes to the back door. Rainwater from the flooded gutter tumbles to the alleyway. He drinks as he stares out at the rain. When the memory of a storm in a distant place grows wearisome, he slips the bottle onto the shelf and pads back to the sofa to lie down again.

The day has left him feeling enraged and out of sorts. It reminds him of his time away. There, then, his mind had been fused shut by fear and his longing for home—his simple struggle to make it through the days. It had been impossible even when he was in it to bridge the world of the Box and the world he knew back home. Here, now, his fears unrealized (although he struggles to remind himself that he *is* alive), he can't find words to tell Charlotte or anyone anything that will make sense. His thoughts drift to all the past confusing and misunderstood emails, the tense phone calls, and as he recalls those things he falls asleep, terrified that he will murder Charlotte again in his dreams.

Sam's crying wakes him. The clock on the microwave says it's close to midnight. How did the hours pass so fast? He goes to the boy's room and finds Sam standing on his bed. The boy's face collapses into a brokenhearted frown when he sees Ludwig.

"I want Mommy."

"Hey, kiddo. Mommy's sleeping. You okay?"

"Change my diaper."

"Okay, okay. We can do that."

Ludwig lifts the boy from the tiny bed and sets him on the floor. He turns on the lamp and strips off the wet bedsheets, takes off Sam's pull-up, and wipes him down. Sam gazes at him evenly, almost curious. Ludwig still feels like a stranger to his own son. He feels as if, like the show he'd been watching earlier, he's been plucked from the Box and placed in another man's home to go through the motions of a strange and unfamiliar life. The hour alarm on his watch goes off, four sharp digital beeps.

"Watch," says Sam.

"Yep."

The boy touches Ludwig's watch, holds up his own arm and looks at his wrist. "Watch," he says again.

Then Ludwig sets on an idea. Where can he find a small toy watch? Where can he find something like that for a boy this young? There must be something with all the Disney stuff, yes? A Mickey Mouse watch! How much can that cost? Can it really be this easy? Yes. He'll give Sam the gift and *finally* win the boy's affection. After various failed offerings—the never-really-touched Marine bear, a menagerie of discarded stuffies, a complicated, age-inappropriate remote control car now hidden away in a closet somewhere—he'll finally give Sam exactly what he's asked for. He grins. "You want a watch, Sam?"

The boy smiles and looks through Ludwig with dream-filled eyes. He's falling back to sleep.

"Mmmm. Mmm. Wanna watch. Wanna watch cartoons."

5.

His old crew are all dispersed. Lorenzo, Gabriel, Lucien, and Ludwig had all once pined to get out of West Philly, to hit some kind of intensely desired but hazily envisioned Big Time. But he sees now that their lives have taken on the contours of necesssity and normalcy.

Lorenzo and his girlfriend, Melissa, had a baby, a little girl named Eva. He's a financial analyst with Wells Fargo, a job that has taken him and his family to Pittsburgh. Lucien lives in Trenton, where he works as a programmer for a company that makes software for health provider networks. And poor Gabriel is dead, killed in 2000, robbed and shot late one night while withdrawing cash from an ATM on Chestnut Street near Drexel. Gabriel's death had been a terrible blow to them all. It had made all of them age all of a sudden.

Something like heartburn singes his chest as Ludwig climbs up the stairs to Mrs. Ávila's apartment. He's come to pay part of the rent. She riffles through the stack of twenties as soon as he hands them over.

"Thees is just three hundred dollar," she says with a frown.

"It's all I've got. I promise I'll bring—"

"You got responsibility, you know?"

"Yes, ma'am. I do."

"I feel awful. When I see little Sam. This"—she holds up the folded wad of bills—"will give you till the end a August."

"Thank you, Missus Ávila."

"It's okay," she says, hand raised. "Is okay. Just do all of us a favor." She backs into her apartment. "Just take care a Sam," she says. "Take care a your baby an your wife."

The door closes. Ludwig backs away, stumbles down the stairs as he fights back tears of shame.

———————

At any time of day, at any point in time, he feels that he wants to be anywhere but where he is. But he knows that this isn't a condition of geography. He's felt for a while a profound displacement. It's self-imposed. It's *wishful*. He feels an urgent jones for—he doesn't know what—a time or place, some object of desire as intense as his need for Go pills in the Box and the shots and pills that Sonia used to give him back in Landstuhl. It matters to him that Charlotte and Sam have left, taken off. It matters to him that each day he confronts an overwhelming inertia. But what matters most—above all those other things—is that they are safe, away from him, and that he is trapped *in this body*.

He, Ludwig, his mind or his soul or whatever the hell it is that's thinking *these thoughts*, is ill-suited to *this person*, this set or collection of memories, this inside-out life or frame of mind in which he finds himself trapped. He wants out. He wants out as badly as he'd wanted out those days and nights in the Box when the whole world felt like one big shit-filled suck. He'd give anything to get his hands on a pill now, a pill to bend the world around him, make it speed up or slow down or simply—most desired—vanish.

———

Summer comes, his favorite season. A heavy heat and humidity descends on the city but it does not clear Ludwig's mind. It does not bring peace.

Lorenzo's mom invites him and Charlotte and Sam over for a July Fourth barbecue. Lorenzo will be visiting home briefly from Pittsburgh.

"It should be fun," Charlotte says, relaying the invitation. She is seated on the sofa, folding freshly dried laundry. She glances up at him as he stands at the sink washing their Sunday-morning dishes.

"Yeah," he says with a smile. "That sounds like fun."

They are enjoying a rare and welcome peace. Their détente for months now has involved a volatile up and down, mostly down. But that sunny day, the weekend a week before Independence Day, is quiet. Sam is taking a nap. At that very moment, they could be mistaken, Ludwig thinks, for a couple whose lives are not upside down.

Charlotte resumes her folding. "I just need you to—" she starts absently.

"What is it?" says Ludwig.

"Just—watch your drinking, okay?"

He bristles and frowns. "What's that about?"

"You know how you guys used to get. Just—" She looks up, and he can see she is trying to be diplomatic. She is trying to avoid a fight, but he's still annoyed.

"That was a long time ago," he says. Since his return from the Box, he has been almost exclusively a secret and solitary drinker.

Charlotte nods, but she doesn't look convinced.

A little later, when she passes him on her way to check on Sam, he reaches out to her and pulls her toward him. He hugs her close, kisses her neck. Feels the warmth of her lithe body against his. He feels her give a little, a rare, passive, bending to his affection. When he looks into her eyes, she smiles sheepishly.

"Don't you feel it?" he says. "Do you know how much I love you?"

"I feel it. " She pulls away with a hesitant smile. "Save it for later."

A week later, at Lorenzo's house, Ludwig finds himself engulfed in the chaos of too many people, too much noise, and too many pressing questions and comments from Lorenzo's well-intended but probing mother, Mrs. Lavalle: "But what are you doing for work?" "Why isn't Sam in full-day daycare?" "But your mother would want you to get a job by now." Etc., etc., etc. Even Lorenzo puts some pressure on after a good, long hug.

"Where you been, man? You layin' low? We hardly see you anymore."

"Whattya mean you hardly see me? You live in Pittsburgh."

Lorenzo is a very big man. Ludwig remembers that when they were kids, in about fourth or fifth grade, Lorenzo started growing so fast that by sixth grade he was the size of an NFL linebacker with a full beard and hair on his armpits and crotch and everything. It was pretty freakish. But now he is a clean-shaven giant of a man, with a round, be-spectacled face and eyes as gentle as Buddha's. He bends close, conspiratorially, and cocks an eyebrow. "What I'm saying is, I hear from my mom that you're not exactly pulling your weight around the house."

The words hurt, but Ludwig knows that that's not Lorenzo's intention. "Shut the hell up," he says.

"Don't knock the messenger. I'm just telling you what I hear." Lorenzo leans back and nudges his glasses up onto the bridge of his

nose. "What's up, man? You know it's *allll* love. *What . . . is . . . up . . .
with . . . you?*" he asks, as he jabs Ludwig's chest with each word.

"I'm just—just trying to get my head back into this. Trying to
figure out the next step."

"Next step?" Lorenzo raises his arms in exasperation. "Come to
Pittsburgh! Why don't you look into finance? Or something like it?
Finish up school? Get your degree. I know it was hard when your
mom got sick, but there's lotsa opportunities. Lotsa choices for a
war hero."

Ludwig frowns and shakes his head. "I'm no hero, man."

"No? Really? You really think that? Look around you, man. This
here is half for Uncle Sam and half for you."

Ludwig glances around Lorenzo's mother's living room. The
party is bursting indoors but has spilled out the front and back of
the house into both small yards. And Ludwig does feel it. He sensed
it as soon as he and Charlotte and Sam arrived, and Lorenzo's mom
made sure that everyone knew they'd arrived, all to rousing cheers
that made Ludwig want to cut and run. Yes, without a doubt, some
of this patriotic pomp is intended for him. But he's not feeling it.
He feels more like a prop than a person, and he resents that he's
been made to feel guilty. He feels that he is taking all the love on
this sunny, bright, and perfect day for granted. He bites his lip. If he
could tell anyone anything, it might be Lorenzo. But the problem is
that he finds himself mute. He sighs.

"Well, I appreciate all this."

"My mom wanted it for you. She's worried about you. Says you're
like a hermit or something. Word is you don't go out much.

Ludwig shakes his head. He is nursing his first beer but pacing
himself. He glances across the room to see Charlotte kneeling
alongside Sam and Eva, Lorenzo's daughter who is now five years

old. The kids are bobbing and grooving to DJ Jazzy Jeff and The Fresh Prince's "Summertime." Ludwig smiles. It feels good to see Charlotte laughing and Sam having so much fun. It strikes him as extraordinary that he and Lorenzo are fathers now. Once they were boys together, free, feckless, but now they are family men with responsibilities and a strange kind of grace because of it. But the feeling grows jagged at its edges.

He turns and looks at Lorenzo. There is one thing that he would like to talk with him about. "Can I ask you something—like, alone?"

Lorenzo, always an observant man, seems to have read his mind.

He hitches his head as a sign to follow him.

Upstairs, in Lorenzo's old bedroom, Ludwig eyes the extraordinary collection of Eagles memorabilia and collectibles, autographed and framed jerseys, posters of Fred Barnett, Brian Dawkins, Seth Joyner.

"Damn, your mom kept all this stuff," he mumbles as Lorenzo rifles through the bedroom closet.

"She wouldn't dare touch it. She knows I'm gonna sell all of it soon enough. Gonna get me some real cash for this stuff." Lorenzo materializes from the shadows of the closet like a genie and hands Ludwig a vial.

"Just a little mix. Don't go gulping it all down." Lorenzo's eyes widen and he rushes across the room. "Put it away," he hisses. He sets his ear to the door. After a while he sighs, breathing heavily. "Jesus."

"Why you so paranoid, man?" says Ludwig.

Lorenzo frowns. "Man, *you* try living with your mother." He frowns nauseated. "Man—Ludwig—I'm so sorry I just said that."

Ludwig feels dismayed. He had not even made any association between Lorenzo's words and his mother's death not so long ago.

"Lorenzo, It's okay man. It's—alright."

Lorenzo breathes a sigh of relief and smiles.

Ludwig holds up the vial. "What is it?"

"A bunch of shit. A little Xanax, a little Valium. Don't go fucking crazy."

Ludwig knows that he's disappointing his friend, but he doesn't know where else to turn. In the years following his father's death by suicide, Ludwig, Lorenzo and Gabriel had sort of lost it, run amok and astray. They'd started doing lots of drugs, boosted stuff and even some cars, scouted the whole town out, as if they owned it. Each likely had a different motivation for those years of wildness. Ludwig had been fueled by a nihilistic fury. He could hardly believe that his father had taken himself away that way. He'd felt as if the bullet had torn through his father's head and into his own heart. Lorenzo, who'd been a dealer for a bit, had grown out of it by the end of high school. Ludwig had gotten out, then relapsed once or twice into bad habits. And of course Gabriel, felled at twenty-one by a random, violent act, never really had a choice in the matter.

Lorenzo shakes his head. "Damn, man. If my mom found out about this—If Charlotte finds out about this—You better keep this shit *tight*."

The stuff—a few pills, from the rattling sound—feels alive, like it's wiggling in Ludwig's palm as he stuffs the vial deep into his pocket. "Thanks, man," he says.

Lorenzo looks down at him. He sets his giant hands on Ludwig's shoulders and shakes his head. "I'm never gonna do this again, so don't ever ask again, okay? I'm doing it now, for old times' sake and 'cause I can see it in your eyes. You need something, but I'm pretty sure it's not this. I wish I knew what it was. Next time I see you, I wanna see you in Pittsburgh, or at school, or working or doin' something worthwhile. You gotta climb outta your head, brother, and join us in the real world. Sam and Charlotte need you. We need you." He glances up at the poster on the wall beside them.

Ludwig looks up too. Donovan McNabb floats frozen forever, football in hand, in the glorious second or two before some spectacular pass.

"The world needs heroes," Lorenzo says solemnly.

Later, after they've returned home, Charlotte retreats with conjugal regrets to the bedroom to comfort Sam, who is fussy and inconsolable at having to leave Eva behind. Ludwig pops a pill, sits back and watches TV. Every now and then he pads to the front window to listen to the shouts and laughter and peer out the blinds to see if he can spot the firecrackers exploding up and down the block. Soon enough he feels whatever is in the pill start to tour through his senses, a welcome, fuzzy feeling. And soon enough he is somewhere else entirely.

A nurse comes in and he sits bolt upright at the edge of the bed. The nurse goes to the credenza and he remembers that he doesn't need to be paranoid. He's not in boot camp. He's not on Parris Island anymore. The nurse sets down a clipboard and a plastic box and goes to the bassinet beside the bed. She gathers Sam up and lifts him to her chest.

"Who swaddled him?" she says.

"I did."

"And this is your first, right?" She sets Sam in his arms.

"That's right."

She smiles at Sam. "I've seen daddies in here three, four times who never got it right."

Ludwig beams. He feels a surge of pride and joy even after two sleepless days. It's this, this thing, in his arms. This little boy. The boy is so light. He's like a cotton ball wrapped in cotton swaddling. He will be fast and nimble. He will fight featherweight. He will lead leaders and part the water.

The nurse smiles over her shoulder. He likes her. Some of the others have hounded Charlotte about breastfeeding, even though she'd had a cesarean and even after the doctor had diagnosed a mild case of pneumonia and told her to stay in the hospital for three more days. But this one's nice. She listens. She comes back from the credenza with a needle.

"Ouch," says Ludwig. He is very much afraid of needles.

"Just a little blood to test for infection. Hold him this way. Hold him firm."

Sam frowns at him and Ludwig can't look away. The boy's eyes furrow as if he suspects something. The furrow softens and his eyes go round. It's more an expression of awe than of pain. The nurse lances a test tube and fills it with Sam's crimson-black blood. Ludwig kisses Sam's eyelids, his plush lips, his nose.

"Ouch," he whispers.

He looks up. Charlotte is standing at the door to the hospital room. The birth was difficult but she looks blissfully happy.

"Daddy did a good job swaddling," says the nurse. "Daddy's gonna do great."

Charlotte beams as she approaches. "I know it," she says.

The mix of pride and joy and expectation Ludwig feels is unlike anything he has ever felt before.

———————

Wandering one night after a bitter argument he discovers near Powelton Village, not far from his place, a bar called the Major Arcana. He has never heard of it or noticed it before. He goes inside, takes a seat at the bar, takes in the big black Jägermeister machine tattooed with crimson Gothic lettering perched at the far end of the massive, brass-bordered mirror, eyes the sparse scattering of patrons who sit still as waxwork statues over drinks that might have been poured half a century ago. He orders one drink, then another and another until he feels all right. The bartender tells him the tavern's stood there since Independence and

Constitution days. Ludwig assumes it's named for some Revolutionary War hero, since everything in Philly is. It's a dive, a greasy little hole perfectly suited to this dingy part of the hood and the desolate sprawl of rail yards that lie just east. He likes it. The place is so deeply marked or infected by a quality of failure and irredeemable cussedness that Ludwig feels right at home. Best of all, he likes the silence.

————

His aunt Jeanette in Gaithersburg, Maryland—his mother's younger sister—phones every now and again to check on him, but the conversations leave him feeling frustrated and angry. He suspects that she is parroting lines and themes fed to her by Charlotte in a badly concealed collusion. He starts to screen his calls, cringes when the phone rings and he sees the Maryland area code.

————

He opens the door, shuts it behind him. The kitchen is barren. There are no toys strewn along the hall. Sam's bed is stripped. Most of the clothes are gone from the closet. Where's the stroller?

On the coffee table, on a slip of paper, Charlotte has written a number Ludwig doesn't recognize. Below it, a note says that she is aware that he fucked around with Shelly that past spring, tells him to stop killing himself with alcohol, and ends with a p.s. that says he can call if he wants to talk to Sam.

Whose number is it? It isn't her mom's. It isn't her aunt's. Paper-clipped to the note are an eviction notice and a clutch of utility, hospital, and credit card bills that total more than seven thousand dollars.

————

At home, or seated on the banks of the river, or hunched over a drink at the bar, Ludwig draws the black sun over and over in myriad variation. He sees it when he closes his eyes, when he opens them, when he thinks of the Box, and when he thinks of Wonder and Ferrer and Vance and the others, which is almost all the time. The black sun dominates the sky of his memories, even in memories from before Fallujah. It begins to become the focus of a strange sort of homespun system, a bit of personal superstition, a kind of customized cosmology centered obsessively on that moment in the sky above Fallujah.

———

At its most intense, when his thoughts are most feverish with it, he feels as if the skin on his face will crack like sunbaked desert soil. What's strangest is that he can't tell if the thing is hot or a brilliant, searing, cold.

———

Worst, most painful of all, is that there's no one to talk to. There's no one to talk to about the thing that he saw, about the Box, about his dead friends. He feels not just alone but alone *in the world.* Like a one-armed man hanging from a cliff, he flails frantically to keep his grip, but he starts to lose it. It gets so the days and nights become an undifferentiated blur. He wakes afternoons to the phantom sound of Sam crying. Nights he hears Charlotte's voice chanting *Wake Up. I need your help. I can't do this alone. I need your help.* And at other times, the worst, he wakes catatonic from dreams in which he is screaming, raging, a monster covered in the blood of his wife, his son, and his long-dead friends.

———

He drinks a little. He drinks too much. He passes out. When he wakes in the dark, *he finds that Vance is passed out beside him. Wonder and Ferrer move slowly around the flames flickering from an oil barrel. Ludwig sits up and rubs his eyes.*

They are in an alleyway and it is night. Marines are sleeping, sitting, gathered all up and down. Ludwig blinks. This could be Al-Khalidiya. It could also be Fallujah, before the beginning. Ludwig crosses his legs and watches. He knows from the way that reality shimmers at its edges that he is far, far gone.

Ferrer and Wonder look far gone too. Ferrer is popping and jerking robotically in a kind of ritual dance, circling the fire. In the dark of night the flames cast red and orange flashes on his sunglasses, and his shadow looms giant against the cinder block walls of the alley. Wonder, on the other hand, moves fluidly; his arms and legs undulate as he orbits the flames opposite Ferrer.

The air smells of burning wood with a toxic taint, an acrid whiff of burning rubber or plastic. Ludwig strains to remember what kind of pills they took. Vance has likely taken twice a dose, as he is wont to do. They are all high as kites.

He watches mesmerized as Ferrer and Wonder move, their two distinct bodies in motion. He laughs, smiles, strains to keep his eyes open. Although he is going into war, he feels so strange and light. He feels at peace. Back home he has brothers from other mothers, but they are very far away, and that time feels long ago. Now he has these brothers whom he has grown to love as he has never loved before, a new kind of love, most intense and unexpected, born in the crucible of duty and pressure and a constant and terrible fear.

Ferrer's dance is a self-parody of the man: clipped, regimented, and hyper-disciplined. For Ferrer has mastered himself. He is all muscle and sinew hewn by sixty push-ups, thirty pull-ups, a hundred jumping jacks, and as many miles as he can fit in each morning before dawn. Ferrer has found in the Marines the perfect antidote to a childhood spent in disorder and disarray. Ludwig and Ferrer share a special, kindred bond. Both their fathers were veterans of Nam. And both Ludwig and Ferrer have shared stories about the cost of war glimpsed in the hollowed-out eyes of their fathers, men who'd lost so much of themselves in a faraway country. When his orbit nears, Ferrer sees Ludwig watching and gently kicks Vance's boot. Vance stirs and sits up. Ferrer motions for them to join in the dance. But at first the two men sit and watch.

Wonder's orbit is loopy and unpredictable, just as the man is. He spins. His legs move Gumby-like, jointless and free. His dance is brilliant and sur-prising. Ludwig frowns to understand what his strange movements mean, for Wonder is the smartest of them, and everything he says is layered and worth deep consideration. Every spare gap in Wonder's rucksack holds a book: on anthropology, on economics, history, science. It is a rare marine who can persuade his buds to act out scenes from Shakespeare. His eyes are closed, but a beatific smile brightens his firelit face. And Ludwig knows how he feels. That knowledge compels him to rise and join in their eccentric and majestic orbits around the jury-rigged star.

Eventually Vance rises too. He starts to move and Ludwig moves beside him, hesitant at first, trying out a way to be distinct from his buddies, something uniquely his own. Vance settles on a martial cadence: his arms swing straight at his sides like a crazed grunt, his boots rise high in a jackboot march, and he juts his square jaw forward as he patrols the perimeter.

Ludwig hears marines of other units, seated or lying nearby, laughing, puzzled at the sight of four men acting ridiculous. But he finds his groove and it feels great. His groove is smooth and syncopated, it's sinuous and free, and he feels so good as he orbits the flames with his buddies, his brothers. He feels so good that he doesn't really mind when he stumbles and hits his knee, opens his eyes, and finds himself dancing drunk and alone in his kitchen in Philly, alone once again in the world.

––––––––

Late one afternoon, seated at the bar in a whiskey-fueled stupor, Ludwig sets down his pen and leans forward to peer at the last of the many black suns he's drawn on a folded piece of paper. *There. There it is*, he thinks. He stares at it and listens close to the higher frequencies humming in his head. That sun, the sun, the boy, his son. Compelled by the vision of his boy and the black sun, he stuffs the paper into his pocket, pays his tab, and bolts out to roam sullen, wind-whipped streets. Finally after much wandering, he walks into a tattoo parlor on Walnut Street.

"What're you interested in?" says the man behind the counter, whose dark blue cardigan, salt-and-pepper hair, and reading glasses looped to his neck make him look more like a librarian than a tattooist.

Ludwig pulls the sheet out of his pocket, presses it flat on the counter.

"Huh." The tattooist squints close. "Interesting. Where you want it?"

Ludwig taps the back of his right hand. "Here," he says. "How much'll it cost?"

The tattooist squints, grasps Ludwig's hand in his, and rubs his thumb across the back. "You sure about this?" He squints over his reading glasses at Ludwig. "Back of your hand's veiny, tender. Lotsa nerves. It'll hurt like a motherfucker. Maybe you might want to come back when you're in a more—sober frame of mind?"

"How much?" he asks again.

The tattooist sighs. "That'd be two hundred. Yeah. Plus tax."

Ludwig blinks, feels that if two hundred dollars and a few days of pain will be the only price to pay, then he has stumbled onto a great bargain. All he wants is once and for all to get the black sun scorched into his skin.

He nods. "Do it."

6.

The phone rings. Ludwig lunges from the sofa. His intention is not so much to discover who is calling as to simply *make—the ringing—stop.*

"Hello?" he says.

"Ludwig? Ludwig is that you?"

"Yeah, that's right."

"Ludwig, how are you?"

"I'm all right." And then, because the voice is familiar, but he isn't sure he wants it to be who it sounds like, he says, "Who is this?"

"It's *me*, Ludwig. It's Sonia."

Ludwig rolls over, reaches down, and gropes the floor. Freaked out, dismayed, he hopes beyond hope there'll be a bottle there, a beer, maybe some whiskey. But his desperate hand finds only empties.

"Ludwig? Ludwig? Are you there?"

He sits up. "Yeah, yeah, I'm here," he says.

"You settling in okay? Easing back into it?"

Settling in, he thinks, as he rubs his face. *Easing.* "Ah. Fuck. You know. It's been all right. A little weird."

There's a pause, a silence that deepens his unease. "You there?" he asks.

"What *happened* was weird," Sonia says. "The way we left things was *really fucking weird.*" Silence. "Ludwig?"

He stares at the floor, mortified. She's decided to confront what he would prefer be left unsaid. And why wouldn't she?

"I—I can explain," he says. "I mean, it's hard to explain. I don't—"

"You don't have to. I just didn't know what happened. I walked into the bathroom and the mirror was smashed in and Otto told me what happened and—"

"But you left. You rotated out. You didn't tell me you were even—"

"I'm sorry," she says. "You seemed so lost. And I felt responsible. Giving you that stuff every day. You were so—I felt like—I don't know. I don't know what I'm saying. Do you understand what I'm saying? Ludwig?"

He sighs, confounded but convinced that she's telling the truth. "Yeah," he says. "I get it."

He hears her breathing and, most disturbing to him, he remembers the heat of her breath against his face, her luxuriant hair cascaded across his chest.

"How's your family? How's your son?"

Ludwig scans the room with haunted eyes. His is a shell of a life, a ruined life. "They're good," he says. "Everybody's good."

"That's so good to hear, Ludwig. I'm so happy you're doing okay. Listen, the reason I'm calling, I wanted to ask you, Ludwig—I wanna know if you might need to make some money. Have you got a job? Do you need a job?"

"Yeah. I mean—yeah. I'm looking. Why?"

"Something came up, and I thought of you. It's great money, if you need it."

"Where are you?" he asks. "Are you in—"

"Connecticut. Stamford, Connecticut."

"Is that— I thought you lived in Jersey?"

"Not really. Not anymore. But I don't live here either. I'm only here for another day. My daughter was at summer camp nearby and I'm picking her up. I'm just—through."

Her voice ebbs in and out. He pulls the phone away, sets it back against his ear.

"I won't be able to see you," she says. "If you come, but I want you to meet someone. She needs—some help. I thought of you."

"Whattya mean? What kind of help?"

"It's hard to explain. On the phone. There's money in it, though. A lot. Are you interested?"

He sets his head in his hand. "Yeah. I'm interested."

"You gotta pen?"

He reaches for the table beside the sofa, finds a pen, and feels a jolt of guilt when he spots on the barrel the name and address of the law firm where Charlotte works. "Okay," he says.

"Okay. Write this down: fifty-two thirty-eight Gibson Road. Stamford. You got it? Ludwig?"

"Got it. But when?"

"As soon as you can."

"What's your—"

"Ludwig? I'm—my cell—Ludwig, are you there?"

Her voice fades in and out. He pulls the phone away, listens again. "What's your friend's name?" he says.

"Stay awake, okay? Just— I just— Keep your eyes open."

"What? Sonia? I don't—What's your friend's name?"

He tries to redial, but each time he hears a ring with no answer. Ludwig sits dazed. He switches on the TV, hoping to find comfort in its anesthetic glow. But he finds as he flips through the stations that there's nothing good on. After a while he turns down the volume, lies back, and watches the blue light flicker on the ceiling. He grips his head. If he can just have one minute's peace, just a few minutes free of the visions, the explosions, the violence, the black sun. He stares at the tattoo on the back of his hand. He closes his eyes.

And what if he can get some cash in hand? What if he can make some money? He could call Charlotte, convince her to come back, convince her that despite everything that's happened, he isn't a lost cause. He opens his eyes again, lies still, and imagines it all play out on the blank screen of the ceiling as he falls asleep.

In the dream he bends to wake Sam, but his son is as stiff as a board and his eyelids are black welts fused shut. Ludwig screams but no sound comes out. When he lifts Sam up, he finds that his little boy's body is weightless, as insubstantial as a saltine. Ludwig turns him over and over in his hands, but he will not come back to life.

He opens his eyes to darkness and waits, curled in a nauseated ball, until he sees the morning light. Then he rises and packs his camouflage rucksack with two pairs of pants, four shirts, and a stack of skivvies. He writes a note to Charlotte and rips it up, writes another and another and another until he comes up with *Charlotte, Had to go but I'll be back. Love, Ludwig.*

He sets the letter on the kitchen table, stares at it a while and thinks of Charlotte and Sam, of how much he wants to give them, of how much he's failed to give them. He figures he's got two weeks to make the rent. When he's ready, he hoists his pack onto his shoulder, climbs the stairs, and walks out into the silver light of an August morning.

7.

It takes five trains to travel from Philadelphia to Connecticut. On the last leg Ludwig eyes with skepticism and a little bitterness the prosperous-looking towns as they roll by, places with strange-sounding names like Pelham, Rye, and Cos Cob. Collapsed in his seat, half asleep, he feels loathsome and lost as his own warm breath deflects back from the window against his face.

When the train arrives in Stamford, it's overcast and threatening rain. He doesn't want to spend money on a cab, so he walks around downtown cadging for directions until he figures out which way to go. He catches a bus that bears him up into hills and woods and suburbs that look so old and respectable, they make him think of butlers and country estates. He gets off and walks the better part of a mile down a blacktopped road edged by a forest of maples and pines. And then he sees it, the address Sonia gave him: 5238 Gibson. A road, or very road-like driveway, leads up to a tree line and a bend beyond which he can't see.

The driveway rises past the trees and the bend to a sprawling ranch house with dark windows set in slate-gray stone. At the top of the flagstone path he finds a sun-shaped knocker hanging on the door. He feels woozy as he raises it. Everything has flowed like a dream for the months leading up to this, as if to this door, to this very moment. He lets the knocker fall.

The door opens. A woman peers out of the darkness. She's Korean, or maybe Vietnamese. She pulls the door open wider.

"Can I help you?"

"I'm Ludwig. Ludwig Mason. I'm—"

"Ah, yes. Missus S. has been waiting for you." She pulls the door open wider. She has on light blue hospital scrubs and pink-and-white running shoes. "I'm Celia," she says. "Come on in."

It's dark inside, shadowed, like the house of an invalid. He smells incense and a faint hint of the sickly funk he remembers from Landstuhl, a whiff of illness and convalescence, of skin struggling against its own decay. He follows Celia across a hall to a dining room. A sweet kind of music is playing: singing, lyrical; a soulful woman's voice chants softly in a language he doesn't recognize. A chandelier hangs low above a long table covered with a mess of books and papers. Across the table sits an old white lady playing a game of solitaire. Behind her a screen, some kind of medical or heart monitor, pulses with green and red and yellow waves that race one another up gentle hills and down steep slopes. A flat-screen TV on a table in the corner is on but muted. An old black-and-white movie is playing. Two cowboys squatting behind a boulder shoot at Indians standing on a ridge. One of the Indians plummets out of view. Beside the TV stands a stacked stereo on which the sharp crimson bars of the equalizer climb and fall to the rhythm of the singer's voice.

"Missus S.," says Celia. "It's Mister Mason, the guy you've been expecting."

"Ah." The woman looks up. She lifts a hand and points to the chair across the dining table. "Sit," she says.

Ludwig sets his rucksack down and sits. He sees that the cards are not arranged for solitaire and that they're not even playing cards, as he first thought. Their faces are decorated with strange symbols, drawings that look familiar, but vaguely so. They're laid out on a diaphanous crimson scarf.

She gestures toward them. "Do you know anything about the tarot? About these cards?"

"I guess I've seen something like them in movies."

"Ah, the movies." She smiles. Coiled locks of white hair cascade over her shoulders. The fabric of her blue robe flows over her, making her seem shapeless. But her hands move fast. She sweeps up the cards, scatters them, and sweeps them up again. Then she starts to shuffle them with the casual grace of an Atlantic City casino dealer. "You know Sonia," she says. "You're friends with her. She trusts you."

"We met in Germany, when I was in the hospital. She called me the other day. Said you need help. Some kinda . . . job?"

"You were in Iraq."

Ludwig glances over his shoulder. Celia stands leaning against the door frame between the dining room and the hallway, watching him. He turns to the old lady. "That's right. I was in the Box."

"The Box?"

"The sandbox: Iraq. Afghanistan."

"Both?"

"No. Me and my buddies, we called the whole thing the Box. I served in Iraq."

"Ah," she says. She stares at him as she shuffles her cards. A crimson pendant, a smooth crystal ball like a drop of blood hangs on a silver chain around her neck. "Would you like anything?" she says. "A drink, maybe? It's so dreary outside."

"Yeah, sure. Please."

"Some whiskey?"

He nods.

"Celia, please bring Ludwig a drink."

Celia goes to the sideboard. The woman, this Mrs. S. across the table, sets the cards down. She smiles absently and he glances at the wall opposite the window. Bookshelves line most of it. A doorway lets onto darkness. Framed photographs cover a small table beside the doorway. The closest is a photo of a young girl who looks like a miniature version of Sonia, sitting, smiling directly at him in the universal pose of a picture-day school portrait. The other photos arrayed behind it are too far away to make out any faces or details. Celia sets the whiskey in front of him.

"Thanks," he says.

Mrs. S. clears her throat and Celia cocks an eye at her. Mrs. S. clears her throat again and Celia mutters something under her breath. She goes to the sideboard and pours a second drink and sets it in front of the old woman.

"I'm not a bartender," she says.

"You should consider it," says the old lady. "Maybe I'd give you tips."

Celia casts a stink eye at Mrs. S. and walks out of the room. Mrs. S. holds her glass aloft. Her sleeve slides up and Ludwig spies a line of gray-blue characters—letters, maybe numbers—a worn tattoo on the parchment of her forearm. She makes a gesture, some wordless toast, and takes a long pull on her drink. She sets her glass down and starts shuffling again. Ludwig sips his drink, but he stops and sets the glass down because he doesn't want her to know how much he wants it.

"Would you like to see how it works?" she says.

"The cards?"

"Yes."

"Yeah. Sure," he says.

She sets the deck on the crimson scarf between them. "I'll do a simple reading. Just three cards. The past, the present, the future. Each card gives you a sense of a different part of your life. Like this—" She pulls a card off the deck and turns it over. It's a spoked wheel, like a wagon wheel, or the wheel of the zodiac. "This is the wheel of fortune."

"What does it mean?"

"What do you think it means?"

"Dunno. Fortune? Fate?"

"Exactly."

"But isn't all this stuff about fate?"

"No. No. This isn't about fate. Nothing's decided here. The tarot works through symbolism, a form of suggestion. It can only tell you what you already know—things that are hidden from you because of consciousness and anxiety. Do you understand?"

"I think so."

She puts the wheel of fortune card back into the deck and hands him the deck. "Take this. You'll split the deck into three separate parts. Take one part and place it here." She points to the scarf. "And from that pile take another and place it here, and then another here."

Ludwig reaches for the deck.

"No," she says. "Use your left hand."

He starts to pull his hand back, but she reaches across and holds it fast.

"What is this?" She squints at the black sun.

"Just something— I got it a few weeks back."

She turns his hand back and forth as if she's studying a gemstone.

"This is—really fine."

"It was a mistake."

"It's unique."

"I was really, really drunk."

"Mistakes can open windows of opportunity."

"I fucking hope so— Ah." Ludwig winces. "Excuse me. It's just—it hurt like hell."

"The ink is set deep." She smiles, sighs, lets go of his hand. "Now split the deck, like I said."

Ludwig takes what he guesses is the top third of the deck, lays it on the scarf where Mrs. S. told him to. He sets a second stack and the last stack beside it.

"You can ask me a question," she says. "Or, if you'd prefer, you can keep the question to yourself. You want to tell me your question?"

"No."

"All right. But you know your question?"

"Yeah."

"Okay. Let's begin."

She slides the top card off the left-most stack and sets it faceup with a decisive flick of her thumb in front of him: the image of a medieval-looking white boy, a country boy, prancing or skipping, looking carefree.

"This is the fool," she says. "This is where we start. It's your past and it's our point of departure. The fool is a symbol of innocence, *your* innocence"—she winks at him—"before you wised up a little. This is a very simple reading. With you, if we used more cards, I'm guessing there'd be a lot more there. There's pain there, darkness—maybe memories of the war?"

Ludwig shrugs. It seems to him an easy guess, so far as guessing at someone's life is concerned. "Maybe," he says.

"This is the present." She turns over the card on top of the middle deck. It bears the image of a heart, a red heart pierced through by three long swords.

"Ah, the three of swords. This is sorrow, a time of struggle. Things aren't so great in your life right now."

She sets her hand on the topmost card of the deck's last third, bends its corner, and glances down. Her eyebrows rise. She looks at him. "You'll see something. Maybe it's the answer to your question. Are you sure you want to see this?"

He nods. She gives him a searching look. Avoiding her eyes, he glances at the swaying pendant before his eyes come to rest on the bent corner of the card under her thumb. He doesn't want to see it. Didn't she say that the cards tell you what you already know? Because he knows that the card will tell him that he's lost Charlotte and Sam forever. How can he get them back if he has destroyed them or they have been destroyed over and over in his dreams?

He stops her hand as she brings it down.

Mrs. S. frowns. "I'm sorry," she says. "Sometimes it's—too much." She sets the card facedown and doesn't break her gaze as she passes her palm over the stacked decks, the two cards she showed him, and the one proffered but not revealed. She mixes them all up irretrievably. Ludwig takes a deep breath and drinks half the whiskey in his glass.

"Thanks," he says.

"Like I said, it's not about fate, it's about choices. For a long time, centuries, these were the cards of a game, like poker or bridge. They were the cards of a game called *tarocchi*. But over time people started using them as occult tools of divination. The cards became popular with royalty. Soon enough, occult practice was common in the courts of empires.

"We've always sought to see the future in things—in the palms of our hands, in the entrails of sacrificed animals, in oils and ashes and tea leaves, in divining bowls, coins, throwing sticks"—her eyes dart upward, conspiratorially—"the stars." She smiles as she flicks some cards faceup into a stack before him. "We're always hoping to see what the next day holds for us, especially when we feel we've lost control. These images"—the last of the cards is the one she set down before, of the boy skipping down a hill—"starting with this one, this one you see here with the zero"—she waves her hand across the stack, and he sees an array of different images, each marked with a roman numeral—"this deck includes twenty-two images that each represent a different archetype—do you know what that means? Archetype?"

Ludwig nods. "Like, an original, right? Like a one-of-a-kind type of thing?"

She purses her lips as she considers his answer. "That's good, yes." She nods. "That works. These images are the heart of the tarot deck." She gestures toward the cards. "These are the major arcana, the *original* symbols."

"The major arcana?"

"Yes."

"Who—who is that?"

She smiles. "The major arcana are not a person. They are these cards I've shown you, in these decks."

"Ah. Jesus. I had—no idea."

Mrs. S. smiles. "Well, enough of this. The point is that games can take on surprising significance. You call those places, Iraq,

Afghanistan, the sandbox, as if they're places where children play. But they're not places to play, are they? It's not a game?"

"No, ma'am. It is not."

"Of course not. It's a serious thing. Those are places where life and death are very much at stake." She slides her hand across the cards again, deftly assembling them back into a stack. "I see this stuff on the TV about Sunnis and Shias, Kurds, people killing one another. People *justifying* killing and murder. And then of course we're there, the United States, American soldiers. Do we even have the right to be there? Killing? Occupying? Who said we could go and invade these places? And people are dying, getting killed by suicide bombs, American bombs. People think other people, *different* people, don't deserve to live here or there, they don't deserve to live at all. So many places in the world, at different times, have seen violence like that, so much tragedy. In Armenia almost one hundred years ago. In Europe, sixty years ago. In Vietnam, Rwanda. Bosnia. I've seen butchery like that with my own eyes."

"Where?"

She hesitates. "I'm part Romany. Did you know that?"

"No, I—didn't."

"Romany, on my mother's side. Udi, from my father. My family came from eastern France, near Alsace. There we were known as *Gitans*. My grandparents on my mother's side, they came from the town of Van, in Armenia. Do you know where that is?"

"No."

"It's in Turkey now, in eastern Turkey. It used to be a big city during the Ottoman Empire. It's where my family came from originally, over a hundred years ago. But they had to flee when the Turks tried to wipe us out during the First World War. A lot of people fled south, to the Middle East, to Syria, and many fled to Europe. My father was an educated man, a poet and a writer, from Yerevan.

It was unusual for Romany to marry outsiders, even now, but my mother was an unusual woman. I come from strong women. In Alsace, the people discovered that my mother was Romany, and my family became known as *les Manouches*. The French called us *Manouches*, or *Gens du Voyage*. In English it's Travelers. Gypsies. You know what I'm talking about?"

Ludwig nods. "Yeah. Yeah. I've heard of Gypsies before."

"When the Nazis came into France, they wiped a lot of people out: Jews, Romany, communists. But you know all this?"

"Some of it. Yeah. A little."

"They sent them to concentration camps and they made them work until they were weak and sick, and then they shot or gassed them. But sometimes they made deals. A Nazi, an officer might see something he wanted: a piece of land, a store or business, a piece of art, even a woman, and he'd say, I'll give you your life. I'll let you live if you give me that. You understand?"

Ludwig nods.

"My family had something a Nazi wanted. It was a deck, a tarot deck that had been in my mother's family for centuries, a deck with twenty-three of these kinds of cards here."

"I thought you said there were twenty-two."

"Ah." She smiles and nods. "You're paying attention. I like that. There *are* twenty-two cards. But this deck—this deck that my grand-mother had, which her own mother had before her and which she gave to my mother—it had twenty-*three* major arcana. It was a leg-endary deck, known to people who *knew*. You understand? Like an open secret." She winks. "People wondered if it really existed. There's even a legend that a woman of my family was summoned to Saint Petersburg to read the fortune of Catherine the Great with that deck.

That set of cards was my family's secret for longer than I know. We didn't *want* people to know about it. It was very unique—too dangerous for people to know about.

"But in France, during the war, a man who knew of these things found my parents. They were young then. My grandparents had died by then, years before the war began. At that time there was my mother and my father and two uncles and three aunts and me and my little brother, Milosh. You're so young. How can you know what it was like back then? But maybe you do know. You've seen war. You might know more about what it was like than I can guess.

"But this was France in 1942. We lived in a small village in Alsace. This Nazi officer came in a big open car with a driver and soldiers on motorcycles. He was handsome, tall with white hair and blue eyes. Eyes blue as the sky, and he was so very polite. He told my mother he'd heard that she was a respected fortune-teller. He asked my parents if he could have his fortune read to him. My mother said yes. She wouldn't have dared to say no. I remember watching from the doorway to the room where I slept at night. My mother sat down with the officer. She took her cards out and started to shuffle them."

Mrs. S. shuffles her own cards. "But before she could start the reading," she continues, "the Nazi, he says, *Can I see these cards?* My mother, she gives him the deck. He lays them out one by one across the table in front of him. His hands move fast, like this." Mrs. S. sorts the cards out in front of her. "He sets aside the minor arcana, these cards here." She piles most of the cards in a stack to her right, and the rest she lines up in two rows in front of her. "Until he gets to the fifty-six cards of the minor archetypes, and then these"—she waves her hand palm down above the ones she's lined closest to Ludwig—"these twenty-two I told you about.

"This Nazi officer looks at my mother and says, *If I walk into a bistro on the Champs-Élysées, and if I order* un aperitif, *my expectation is that the* garçon *will offer me the choice of the best, if I can afford it. Is that not so, madame?*

"My mother, she looks at him and she says, *But of course.*

"The officer says, *But, madame, if you agree with me, then why have you not given me a choice? Why have you presented me no choices?*

"My mother was confused. She said, *I do not understand. There will always be choices. I am not telling you your fate, only what you can* choose *to do with your destiny.*

"And the officer," she continues. "He says, *No, madame, you misunderstand. I know very well of the practice of the occult. That's not what I'm talking about. I am talking about this tarot deck.*"

"My mother must have sensed that she was dealing with someone far more dangerous than she first understood. She said, *I don't understand. What do you want from me?*

"The officer pointed to the deck and said, *There are only twenty-two major arcana cards in this deck. Where is the twenty-third card?*

"My mother looked at him. It's possible that at that moment everything was already decided. Maybe something in her eyes told him that what he wanted, what he had come to get, wasn't just a rumor or legend, but a real thing."

Ludwig's eyes dart to the glass of whiskey, but he also feels like he might throw up. Mrs. S.'s heart rate on the monitor is moving fast, and his own heart follows. "What happened?"

Mrs. S. sighs. Her gaze is mournful. "She tried to deny that she knew anything about a deck with twenty-three cards. But it was too late. He knew the truth. He had the soldiers who had come with him destroy our house, the walls, the furniture and beds, until they found it."

"They found it? Where was it hidden?"

"It was in a little red box that my mother kept hidden under the floorboards, under her bed. It was hidden in a secret drawer in the bottom of that box."

"What happened then?"

"The officer took it. Maybe it would have been different if my mother had given him the deck willingly. Maybe not. I don't know. He had all of us, my mother and father, me, Milosh, our cousins and their parents, my uncles and aunts who all lived nearby, taken away. They sent us to the camps. Most of us were sent to Natzweiler-Struthof, near Strasbourg. Some of us were sent to Dachau. I was sent to Natzweiler."

"Jesus."

"Yes, they exterminated my family, almost all of us. One of my cousins, Aishe, survived Dachau, and I survived too. I was orphaned, and then I moved to Paris and then, soon after the war, to Montreal."

"My God." Ludwig feels shaken. He's been swept up in her story, and its ending leaves him feeling desolate. "How did you—go on?"

"Go on?"

"With your life? After all that?"

"Ah, well. Not so well. When I was young, I was obsessed with what had happened to my family. When I lived in Montreal, I had no connections to anyone. I felt disconnected from the world, even from myself. I knew that my cousin, Aishe, felt very much as I did. She was so restless. She moved everywhere, to Ireland, South Africa, Morocco, Argentina. She married a Moroccan man in Casablanca. She had a family there. I heard from her only every few years.

"In Montreal, I had a lot of different jobs, but, God, I was a terribly lonely person. Then I met a young American man. He worked for the Sun Insurance Company in Montreal. He lived in my building and we fell in love. But it was hard at the start. He could see that I was heart-broken. He couldn't stand to see me suffer. He loved me but he knew that I needed some kind of help. The world is a different place after war, even after the violence stops. He told me I should look for the parts of my life that I had lost. He said I could save myself by looking for what had been taken from my family. And so I decided," she continues, "that I would find this deck of twenty-three cards. I would find it and maybe save a part of what had been lost. You understand?"

He nods. His mouth is dry. "I think so. But there's a big difference between some cards and the people you lost."

"Yes. There is. But I had a mission. Soon after I made this decision Henry moved back to New York. He said he would wait for me. Then I traveled to Germany. Everything that followed after that felt inevi-table, even to this very moment in which you're sitting here. I went to Munich and I started to research to find out about this Nazi officer who took the tarot deck from my family."

"What did you find out?"

"His name was Fritz Hollenbach. He had been a devotee of the occult, an avid collector. At the end of the war he was shot by Rus-sians in Berlin, not far from the Reich Chancellery. His oldest son, a teenage boy, was a Nazi youth, and he was killed, too, around the same time. But the younger son and the mother, I couldn't find any trace of them. And I couldn't find out what happened to his property, including the deck that Hollenbach stole. I gave up hope. How could I find a tiny deck of cards in Munich? In all of the world?

"But one day, by chance, I read in a newspaper that an Englishman had bought at an auction some property seized from officers after the trials of Nuremberg. The man was named Benjamin Colwyn. Do you know that name?"

"No."

"Colwyn is well-known in occult circles. He died soon after the war. And after he died, many of his belongings, including his collection of occult objects, were auctioned. They were auctioned to collectors all over the world. Many of the buyers purchased items anonymously." She takes a pull on her drink, stares absently at the cards laid out in front of her. "So I gave up then. I felt I would never be able to find the deck."

"What did you do?"

"I went home. I went back to Montreal and I made arrangements to come to the United States, to be with Henry. I had failed to do what I had set out to do, but I felt that maybe I could start to live a normal life, to enjoy life with Henry. Maybe everything that had come before might be forgotten." She stares at something in the middle distance, a memory hovers unseen but sensed by Ludwig just between them. The waves on the heart monitor behind her climb, drop fast, climb, climb, drop, just as his own pulse climbs, plummets, strains to recover, and drops again. "I could have a life, something of my own after all that was taken away." She pauses, gazes at the table again, and for a moment Ludwig wonders if she's passed out with her eyes open. "And I found it," she whispers. "I found the love I needed."

The siren on the monitor goes off.

"Hey!" Ludwig says, panicking. He gets up, backs away from the table, leans into the hallway. "Hey! Celia!"

Celia rushes up the hall and into the dining room. She sets her hand on the old woman's shoulder and taps at the monitor. The siren stops. The waves start to calm.

"Sweetheart," Celia whispers into Mrs. S.'s ear. She strokes her silver hair, kisses her on the forehead. She goes to the curtains and casts them wide open. It doesn't do much good. It's dismal outside. All the while Mrs. S. gazes at the cards with a look of deep mourning.

Ludwig doesn't want to stare, so he keeps his gaze away. Even under all that gray, the leaves of some of the trees at the edge of the property glow bright green. Celia bends to his ear as she passes. "Keep an eye on the monitor," she whispers. "Don't let her get so excited, okay?" She leaves the room and Ludwig waits. Finally Mrs. S. looks up at him and blinks.

"You—okay?" he says.

"Yes." She frowns. "Why do you ask?"

"Ah." He sets his hands on the table. He waits a moment. "So, you never found the deck."

She looks at him, sighs, and sips her drink. "No. I waited one year, then two years. Decades passed, and I was happy. Then, after Henry died a few years ago, I decided that I needed to look for the deck again, before *I* died. I started where I left off. Celia helped me find things." She grins. "The internet is fantastic! I found some leads, and then"— she pauses—"I think I found the box," she says breathlessly. She looks over his shoulder. "Celia. Celia where are you?"

Celia comes in.

"Celia, would you get me the envelopes? And the book?"

Celia takes a large manila envelope, a white business-size envelope, and a book from the table beside the TV and sets them in front of Mrs. S. She leaves the room. On the spine of the paperback Ludwig sees the title *The Origins of the Occult Tarot*. As Mrs. S. undoes the twine that secures the flap and riffles through the manila envelope, Ludwig pulls the book toward him and studies the ornately designed cover, the copper-colored lettering of the title.

"Here," she says, handing him two sheets stapled together. "Look at this."

They're black-and-white photocopies of a page from a book or catalog that show two pictures, one from the front and one from the side, of a box with two drawers covered with curving patterns. The pull handles on the drawers are shaped like the faces of birds, maybe falcons. The caption reads: *Ottoman. Van or Vostan. c. 11th century. Wood and inlaid mother of pearl.*

"What are those?" he says, holding the sheet up and pointing to the drawer handles.

"The handles represent the Egyptian god Thoth."

He sets the sheet down. "Did you find out who bought it?"

"Ah, right. That's the question, right? *Who bought it?* Things got interesting." She takes a long pull off her whiskey. "I have no idea. I only know that someone bought it in 1957, at an auction. That person paid 336,000 dollars for it. But it hasn't been seen since."

"For this?" He glances at the pictures of the box. "No offense, but that's a lotta money."

"Yes. Yes, it is. But that's not the value of the box and it's certainly not the value of the deck that may be inside it. Do you know how they say that people know the price of things but not their value? The deck has no price. It's beyond price."

Ludwig blinks, skeptical. The box looks like—a box. "Do you think whoever bought it knew what it was? Did he think or know the deck was inside it? Is that why he bought it?"

"I don't know. I mean—why pay so much for it unless he knew what it was? I believe the person who bought it knew its value and paid the price he needed to in order to get it. It's possible that other people who wanted it couldn't afford it."

"So—it's not really a secret?"

"What?"

"The deck. People know about it."

"*Yes. Yes*, like I said, it was a thing of legend. That's why it was taken from us."

"So someone has the deck? But you don't know who?"

"Yes, that's right. But I do know *something*. I believe I know where this person *lives*. And that's what I told Sonia. That's why Sonia told me about you. That's why you're here—why *you* came *here*."

Maybe it's his expression. Maybe it's the long silence that follows that prods her to explain:

"I want you to find the tarot deck that was taken from my family. I want you to find it and bring it to me."

Ludwig sits up. He didn't know what he had expected, but he hadn't expected this. "Listen, ah, Mrs. S., right? I don't know what to say. When Sonia called, she said— Listen, I'm just looking for, like, a regular-type job. That's what I thought Sonia was talking about. I—I *had* a job, but it didn't work out. I've got a wife, a kid. I need—"

"Money."

"That's right, yeah. Exactly."

"I understand. Sonia told me. I wouldn't ask you to do this without paying. Sonia told me I can trust you."

"Is Sonia—in on this?"

"But of course. Why else would you be here?"

"But— I'm— Help me out. How do you and Sonia know each other?"

She looks surprised. "Sonia is my grandniece. She's Aishe's grand-daughter, my cousin, who I told you about, who survived Dachau. Aishe married a Moroccan man. Actually, to be honest, I don't know if they actually ever legally married—"

"Ah, weird. This is all—kinda coming together."

"The girl there"—she points to the framed photo of the girl on the table beside the doorway—"that is Rania, Sonia's daughter." She smiles. "Rania spent her summer nearby, at a summer camp in

Cornwall. Then I had her here with me for five days. Five good days." Her smile fades and she turns to him. "They are my family. They are the only family I have left in the world. Sonia told me that I can trust you. She said you're a good man with certain—talents. She thinks you can do this thing for me."

Ludwig hesitates. "Well, that's nice of her to say, but that's not really the point. I'm not like a— I've got no idea where to start. I'm a— Listen, I was just a marine, you know, a jarhead. I've been— well, ah, I was in college before that. I was at Temple, doing comp sci, but, well, my mom got sick and it didn't work out. Two years and almost a half of school. But my mom, she just— I had to take care of her. Then I had a job working as a vendor, in Philly, at Veterans Stadium, but I was having trouble making ends meet. So I started working for this company that manages parking lots. Anyway, I was making, like, a thousand a month. And no benefits. I was goin' no-where. You know what I mean? Then, my fucking boss— excuse me. This asshole calls me out for boostin' cars. That's right, framed. Anyway, lawyer says I should plea and when I'm on probation, I just figured I had nothin' to lose. So I signed up. Went to Parris Island, and then Charlotte and I— Did I mention her? That's my wife— we got married. The war started, and then my son was born. And I was a corporal, a marine corporal. I manned the fifty cal on a Humvee. My mom died. Breast cancer. But I'm back now. Just trying to settle in. I had a job at a SaveRight, in Philly, but I got— Well, there was some trouble and I had to go. The short of it is I'm not like a— I don't know what you'd call it. Maybe you could just contact who-ever it is you think bought the thing? Right? Direct, and just tell him you feel you need some kinda compensation? Yeah? Or— Hey, how about a private, like, investigator? Or maybe a lawyer?"

Mrs. S.'s look of concern makes Ludwig hesitate.

Embarrassed, he sits back and takes a deep breath. "Short of it is, Missus S., I really don't know how to do what you're asking. I'm just looking for a real job. Something that'll give me skills development, and'll look good on my résumé. Like a security job. With health benefits. That kinda thing."

"Would you do it for fifty thousand dollars?" she says.

He frowns. "What? You mean five thousand?"

"No. No. *Fifty, fifty* thousand dollars."

"For a *year*?"

"No. No, for the job. For this one thing."

Ludwig looks into Mrs. S.'s eyes. But she doesn't blink. He reaches for his drink and finishes it off. "Yeah," he says. "That would work."

Mrs. S.'s face brightens with the broad, earnest grin of a child. "How do we start?"

"I'd need money. Like a deposit. Cash. You know. Now."

"Okay, I can give you something. I can give you an advance. What if I give you part of the money? What if I give you five thousand dollars? Would that work for you?"

"Can you make it seven?"

She sighs, nods. "Yes, I can give you seven thousand. That will work for you?"

"Yeah. Yes. Definitely. Thank you. Thank you." He closes his mouth and watches her, wary that another word will reveal him as stone-cold green in every way.

Mrs. S. opens the white envelope and pulls out a stack of hundreds that Ludwig eyes with a woozy surge in his chest that feels like heartbreak. She counts out seventy with the same ease with which she's dealt the cards and pushes them across the table.

"This is to pay your expenses, while you're doing this thing. You think this'll be enough?"

"Yes." He folds the cash in half and puts it in his pocket. "Thank you." He sets his hands on his knees under the table so they won't betray him. "I've never done anything like this before," he says. "Not sure how to start."

She nods, pulls a yellow sheet of paper out of the manila envelope, holds it up to her face. "Here. Yes. Look at this." She pushes the sheet toward him. In the middle, in a cursive, elegant hand, is written: *357 Chatham Street, Mobile, Alabama.*

"Alabama?"

She nods. "Mobile, Alabama." Her eyes are bright and wide. She sets her finger on the address. "You can go to this house in Alabama. I'll pay you. I'll pay you the rest of the money, another forty-three thousand, if you go to this house and get the deck. Bring it back to me here."

"Go to this house. Knock on the door. Ask for it."

She gazes at Ludwig. The brightness in her expression fades a little under a cloud of sudden doubt. "If that's—the way you choose, then yes. Sonia told me you would know what to do. Maybe some other way might be better if you find that whoever has the deck is— reluctant to return it."

Ludwig nods with a shadow of pity in his heart. As odd as she is, it feels weird to see an otherwise respectable-seeming old lady sanction breaking and entering. "Okay. So you really think whoever lives there has got this deck?"

"I do. All roads lead to that house."

Ludwig looks her in the eye. He guesses that if he does it fast, if he doesn't waste time, he can just get on the train and head back to Philly and pay Mrs. Ávila what he owes. Mrs. S. doesn't look like she'll be around to moan over it for long, anyway, and maybe he won't feel so guilty about it in a week or two. So, what the hell? "All right," he says. "I got it. Get it. Take it—whatever it takes. Bring it here."

Her eyes brighten again. "Good. Good. I'm so happy. And I'll be even happier when I can see it."

He hesitates, but when he realizes she's done, he rises. "It was good to meet you."

"Sonia has spoken so highly of you. It sounds like you are very dear to her."

Ludwig nods and wonders what Sonia told her. She must've spotted him or suspected him after the dispensary thing in Landstuhl. That would explain her calling him for this job. But did she say anything to Mrs. S. about his shakes and convulsions? Did she say how he'd begged for Go pills? Did she tell Mrs. S. that he'd betrayed his wife with her? Did she say he'd punched out her bathroom mirror and left a bloody mess behind?

"Celia," Mrs. S. calls. "Celia, where are you? Please show Ludwig to the door."

Ludwig hoists his rucksack onto his shoulder, turns to leave, and stops. "Hey," he says.

Mrs. S. looks up from her cards.

"Have you looked in the cards?" he asks. "For all of this you want to do?"

"Of course. I wouldn't do this if the cards didn't look right."

"So you'll get what you want?"

She sighs. "I told you already, these won't tell me or you or anyone what will happen. The cards can only suggest a course, like—like options." She glances up at the heart monitor. "I don't need these cards to tell me what's ahead for me. And when I look at the past, I know I've seen much of the worst and much of the best. I've gotten what I needed most from my family, who I lost, and from Henry, who came into my life when I most needed love and light. I've seen a lot in my life. As for this card, this twenty-third card, I just want to know what it is, what it might mean. This is how I hope to redeem myself."

"*Redeem* yourself? But—you didn't do anything wrong."

"Yes." She looks at him. "I did. I survived. I lived while the others did not. Worst of all, I lost the legacy that would have been entrusted to me. I don't know what's in those cards. I don't know what symbol is on that card, but I *must find out*."

"But you had it? Right? I mean, when you were a kid, you saw it?"

"Yes, but I didn't care. I was a child, but I still feel ashamed about it. I knew that there was something special about it, but I didn't care. All I cared about was the box it was in, the little box that held my mother's earrings, her jewelry, her bracelets and rings. *Those* are the things I remember. The things I coveted, like a child, like a child that doesn't know what's most important, what needs to be protected most. I didn't know. But now I know. This is what I want.

"I've studied the tarot almost all my life. Because my mother was taken from me, I know only what I learned by myself. I've tried to remember what the card could be. What that symbol could be. I've read, studied. But there is almost no trace of the deck. The deck has vanished without a trace. Does that mean that my family's legacy will vanish too, when I die? That centuries of wisdom will be lost? Is it a key? Does that symbol say something about what we are or *who* we are? Could the symbol on it help us to understand ourselves better? I want to see it, to know what it is, before I die."

Ludwig nods. "Well, if it doesn't sound too, ah—self-centered, how about for me? What's it look like for me?"

"We didn't finish your reading, remember? You didn't want—"

"But *you* looked. You saw what was on that last card. You—"

"*Ludwig*, remember what I said? It's *not* a crystal ball. I can't tell you what you already know. This is about *choices*."

"But what—what choices, do I have?"

She sighs, shrugs, splits and riffles the deck in her hand. "Maybe I can help you with that one. I saw a glimpse of something, but not in the cards. You have a big choice you'll need to make very soon. You can choose to do what you're thinking of doing, taking my money and vanishing. Or you can do what you promised." She looks up and winks. "*That's* your choice."

He blinks at that. Because she seems to have seen or understood so many things about him, he isn't surprised that she saw that too.

"I wasn't going— I just need some time to think about this."

She raises her eyebrows. "How much time?"

"Not much. Just give me the day."

She nods. "A day? I can live with that. Have a good day, Ludwig."

He turns, hesitates, turns back. "This stuff, here"—he gestures to the envelope with the papers and the book—"can I borrow these?" He notices that the white envelope from which she had pulled the cash has vanished.

"Yes, please do. We put these things together for you."

"Thanks." He gathers up the book and the envelope and stuffs them in his rucksack.

On the way out, Ludwig asks if he can use the bathroom. Celia leads him through a kitchen, where he spies a TV with a soap opera on, water boiling in a saucepan on the stove, white wicker furniture in a sunroom beyond sliding glass doors. In the bathroom he pisses, washes his hands, and then rifles through the medicine cabinet until he finds, bingo, a bottle with a prescription label, made out to one Nikita S. Thorpe of 5238 Gibson Road, for thirty doses, 10 milligrams each, Supeudol. Three weeks' worth of little beige-colored oxyco-done pills. He puts the bottle in his jacket pocket.

When Celia opens the front door, Ludwig steps out. Rainwater drips from the eaves. He gazes at the drizzle under the strange white sky.

"Missus S. is a character, huh?" says Celia. "A little *loco*, huh?"

"Huh. Yeah. She's a—pretty interesting. Hey, ah, is she—is she gonna be all right?"

"Oh, I can't say. She's strong." Celia shakes her head. "But— I can't say. Hey," she says. "Don't you have an umbrella?"

"No. I'll be okay. Thanks."

He walks down the flagstones and glances back. Through the front window, past the rivulets of rain that dribble down the glass, he glimpses Mrs. S., amber lit in the shadows of her dining room, bent over her cards. Celia steps to the window and squints at him. He feels all of a sudden like she's caught him spying. He starts to raise his hand to wave, but before he can even smile she draws the curtains closed.

8.

He walks up the road to the bus stop and sits. He fumbles for the bottle of Supeudol in his jacket pocket and swallows one dry. He waits. Finally he pulls the cash out of his pocket and counts it to make sure it's real. It's real. He pulls out the book and the envelope, riffles through the thick sheaf of photocopies of excerpts from books, photos, lists. They're real too. But what if he's being set up? What if the whole thing's a scam? What's the scam, though? And what's in it for them? Unless she wants something that's a lot more valuable than she said? Maybe Sonia and this Mrs. S. are in on it together?

The rain stops and the street starts to bend. He looks one way and the other and quickly loses his sense of left and right. His head spins from the oxy and from all the stuff Mrs. S. said, this thing she's asked him to do, the money, the money, the wad of good clean money in his pocket. He gets antsy and starts to worry that he could wind up waiting there forever. So he sets off along the shoulder.

Half an hour later he walks into a gas station along an otherwise desolate stretch. The store spins around him and he tries not to act too anxious or edgy. Every time Ludwig looks away, he's sure the attendant is glaring at him over the edge of his newspaper. Ludwig picks up a prepaid cell phone, a ham sandwich, a roast beef sandwich, two mini-cans of cheddar-flavored potato chips, a bag of salted peanuts, two cans of soda, a bag of teriyaki-flavored beef jerky, and a mini-pack of Twinkies.

He sits at a picnic table outside and breathes deep the fumes of unleaded gas and windshield wiper fluid as he eats the ham sandwich, drinks the sodas, and wolfs down the Twinkies and the peanuts. When he's done, he stuffs what's left in his pack and looks up. Through the store window he sees the clerk stocking a refrigerator with a rainbow array of thirst quenchers—pink and yellow and orange and red and blue, side by side, row by row, just as methodically as Ludwig used to line up ammo and gear at his side up top of the Humvee in the Box when they had been headed into the shit.

He closes his eyes and focuses on forgetting. When he opens them again, he pries the cell phone from its packaging and fiddles with it until he figures out how to activate it. He has kept in his wallet the phone number Charlotte left in her goodbye note. So he dials the number now. The phone rings. Then:

"Hello?"

His heart climbs fast, fist over fist up his throat. It's her. It's Charlotte.

"Hello?" she says again.

"Charlotte, it's me. It's Ludwig."

There's a pause, then, "Ludwig. Oh. Oh, Ludwig—" she says. Her voice, her voice, she sounds so close. He feels like he can almost touch her, like she's only a few feet away, like if he can just reach into the phone and stretch his arm a little, he might touch her cheek and whisper to her that everything will be okay, if he could just—

"What do you want?"

He hesitates. The parking lot, the gas station, the whole thing is shimmering and spinning and he wishes he hadn't taken the pill. "Is Sam there?" he says.

"Hold on."

Ludwig hears voices, a sound like a chair leg dragging across linoleum. He strains to imagine the space they're in. If they're at her mom's, are they in the kitchen? Are they in the den with the big brown leather easy chair?

"Hello, Daddy."

"Hey hey, Sam."

"Daddy."

"Little buddy."

"I come home?"

"Yes. Come home. I mean—wait for me, then I'll call for you, okay? I've just gotta get some stuff done, okay? Then we should all just meet at home. Okay? Meet me home?"

"Meet home?"

"Meet you at home. See you at home. I love you, monkey. I love you so much."

"Daddy." Sam sounds genuinely happy, which thrills Ludwig. The boy's exhilarated breath fills his ear.

"Are you done?" It's Charlotte's voice. Ludwig hears a struggle, Sam whining. "You're done now. Give me the phone, Sam. Give it to me. Come back here. Sam. Give it. Give it to me now." There's a long pause. Then, "Is there—anything else?" she says when she gets back on the phone.

"I—" Flustered, Ludwig hesitates.

"Listen, I—" she starts.

Silence.

"I'm working on the bills," he says. "Rent's covered through August. But I'm working on getting the money for the other stuff. I got a job. I—"

"Ludwig."

"I mean, not a job exactly but—"

"Ludwig."

"What?"

"It's not about the money."

He stops. The spinning stops too. "Then what's it about?"

"It's about us."

He squints, listens closer. Is she crying?

"I'm so sorry, Ludwig, I waited so long for you and maybe I expected too much but I didn't expect this."

"*This?* What? What's *this?*"

"What's this? This is *nothing*, Ludwig. *Nothing*. This is you staring at a blank TV screen. This is you fucking around with Shelly, Ludwig. *Shelly*. Did you really think I wouldn't find out?"

"Jesus, Charlotte, I—"

"No. No. No. You shut up and let me talk. This is you *screaming*, Ludwig, *screaming* for your life in the middle of the night. This is you holding your son—your *son*, Ludwig—and staring at him like you're trying to figure out who he is."

"I know. I know. I just—"

"And the drinking. Ludwig."

"I'll stop. I swear. I'll—"

"Do you want him to grow up around that? I mean, do you want—"

"Jesus Christ, I said I'll stop. I just—"

"'Cause I don't want him around that."

"I know. I know."

"I just wish we could start over."

Her words stun him. They've had it out plenty over the past half year but now she's laying the whole thing out for them both to see, plain and honest. He closes his eyes and crouches. "I know, but we can't. I can't," he whispers.

He listens to the long silence. He wants to ask her why he feels so hollow inside, so emptied out. And he knows he can't ask her why he wants to hold her in his arms one minute and slam her in the face the next. He wants to ask her if he'll ever feel normal again.

"You can call him again if you want."

"Okay, okay, but what about—"

"What?"

"Us? What about you and me?"

Charlotte is quiet. "I don't know—" She goes silent, then, "I have to go."

"Okay."

"Bye."

"B—"

She hangs up. Ludwig rises, shouts in rage at the sky, and throws the phone. It skips and spins into the road, and because the road is spinning now, too, it loops away and then back. He watches it spin for a while before he heads across the lot to pick it up. A semi comes around the bend. He steps back but it crushes the phone. *Fuck*, he yells. A bus follows right behind. Its front wheel rolls over the shattered pieces. The driver opens the door.

"You getting on?"

Ludwig takes a deep breath. "Gimme a sec."

He grabs his pack, climbs on, and takes a seat at the back as the bus pulls away from the curb. He strains to hold himself together, but he's sweating and out of breath and he can't keep his hands from shaking. He clenches his eyes shut and when he opens them, he watches *the crowd of boys running along the side of the road, passing a soccer ball like pros, waving, laughing, Tikrit beyond them. Two Chinooks, landing in the field nearby, kick up thick clouds of dust. But they keep laughing, all of the running boys, as Ludwig cranes his neck to watch them get swallowed up by the dust.*

By the time he gets off the bus it's late. He asks around for a bookstore and a game store, hoping he might get his hands on a tarot deck, but it turns out both are closed. Then he walks the half mile from downtown to a dingy motel, where he finds a room for thirty dollars a night, and to his great relief a kind of bar-slash-liquor store just next door to it stocked with fortified wine, cheap whiskey and schnapps, and unrefrigerated cases of Keystone Light and Pabst Blue Ribbon beer. He exercises restraint and buys a six-pack of Pabst and a fifth of bourbon.

Back in his room, he eats the leftover roast beef sandwich, crushes a can of warm beer down his throat, drinks a good portion of the whiskey, and eases into the last sad stretch of the afternoon's regrettable high. He stares at the open bathroom door and beyond it the shower curtain and the shower rod. He thinks, *If I had the guts I could just—* But the idea doesn't come together. He doesn't want to think it through. He's afraid to think it through. He remembers how, even as they'd pinned the medals on him back in California, he'd thought the real act of courage was the thing he was too afraid to do. And how would he do it? How will he do it? With his belt on the rod? With a hook in the closet?

His father had done it with a bullet. Ludwig wonders if his father had felt this way, too, for all those years leading up to that day. He remembers a Christmas morning when he was a kid when he had discovered his father asleep on the sofa with a spilled bottle of whiskey clutched in his arms and his beloved Beethoven— Ludwig's namesake—a late string quartet, the 131, playing like a dirge evoking violent trauma and unfulfilled promise on the turntable Ludwig wasn't really supposed to touch but sometimes did when no one else was home. (And he remembers, too, that ongoing, never-ending debate with his father, over music, over the meaning and merit of different kinds of music, and his frustration that he could never convince his father that Public Enemy or Wu-Tang might be as worthy as Beethoven or Mahler, Sam Cooke or Nina Simone. His father's argument was that time might change a lot of things, but that the traits that make some things compelling and authentic were bound in mastery of craft and eternal.) Even then Ludwig knew, or guessed, that his father had done those things—the drinking, the restless nights and zoning out—not because of an illness or weakness, but because he'd gone through something indescribable too—Vietnam—and although that didn't excuse everything, it excused a lot of things. And for Ludwig, at least, if not for Ludwig's long-suffering mother, it had helped excuse or explain why his father had been absent in spirit even when he had been physically present, and why he had looked so often as if he'd just woken up to find himself stranded in yet another dream. It had helped excuse even his suicide.

Ludwig cups his face in his hands and thinks of what Mrs. S. said about how ridiculous a thing it was to consider after everything she'd been through. Finally, although he's planned to hold off, maybe even flush the pills away, he finds himself holding the bottle of oxycodone and staring at the label. He tries to clear his mind and let the silence wash over him, but Sonia's voice pierces in: *Stay awake. Stay awake*, and he puts the vial in a pocket of his rucksack. He lies on the bed and stares at the ceiling, focused on the remembered sound of her voice repeating the mantra over and over again.

9.

He sits at the edge of the bed and watches the morning creep in along the edges of the blinds. He looks askance at the empty cans, the half-empty bottle on the nightstand. The memory of the dream and thoughts of Charlotte and Sam rouse the ache inside him. The remnants of the oxy feel like a hangover, a dreadful mistake, a cramp of mortification and regret deep inside his soul. He doesn't want to face the light of day if it might expose the darkness inside him.

He feels as if time is passing fast. It'll be too late unless— He musters the strength to rise, root through his pack, and pull the folded sheet of yellow paper from the envelope Mrs. S. gave him. He unfolds it, lies back, and stares at the address scrawled inside: 357 Chatham Street, Mobile, Alabama.

He'd given Mrs. S. nothing and yet she'd given him the cash. She'd even told him she suspected he might take it. And yet she'd given it to him anyway. And then there was Sonia. He didn't know her well but he *knew her*, instinctively, in some strange familial way. They'd both seen things.

Could it really be so easy? Find a way to get it, take it if he has to, bring it back to her. He thinks of fifty thousand dollars: $50,000, with the sign and the five and the four fat zeroes. It seems—impossible. Ludwig stares up at the ceiling and thinks of those zeros signifying space, an oval of surprise on Charlotte's lips. And, come to think of it, a zero-shaped pool for her and Sam. He crosses his hands behind his head and thinks of all the things the zeroes can buy and be.

He wakes in the afternoon and stands in the shower. *Time to go*, he thinks. The money's the only reason he needs. It's time to head to Mobile. He feels focused and mission oriented. He's going to go with this and see it through. Same as deciding to sign up. Same as getting through the burn of Parris Island. Same as the Box.

He picks up the phone on the nightstand and calls the number written on the manila envelope Mrs. S. gave him.

"Hello?"

"Yeah, is this Celia?" he says.

"Ludwig?"

"That's right. Can you tell Missus S. I'll do what she asked? I'll do the job."

There's a pause. "Yes. Thanks for calling. She's been cranky. She'll be happy to hear this."

"No problem. Bye." He hangs up.

He eats at a diner downtown, stares out the window at the quiet silver day and the people walking along the street. He plans to take a bus, but at the Amtrak station he changes his mind and picks a train, a red-eye, all stops. He pushes some of the fresh, crisp bills that Mrs. S. gave him under the bulletproof glass.

"One way? Or round trip?" says the clerk.

"One way."

Ludwig takes a seat near the back of the train car, near the bathroom stall. As he settles in he feels a painful longing for the lost, the dead all stuck back there in the past forever. He looks at the tattoo on the back of his hand, and as he dwells on that day and that last moment in the sky outside of Fallujah he misses the last glimmer before the sun recedes, dims, and vanishes beyond Stamford, Connecticut.

10.

The floor-to-ceiling windows of the Amtrak station in downtown Mobile face east over the brown waters of what an old man in a green porkpie hat tells Ludwig with a look of withering contempt is *not* the Mississippi River, as Ludwig guessed, but an estuary of Mobile Bay.

When the doors slide open, Ludwig winces at heat so intense, it reminds him of secondary blasts from ordnance back in the Box. He hails a cab, and the driver recommends a motel near the Civic Center a few blocks away. A vicious-looking scar runs from the crown of the cabby's short-cropped head to the middle of his cheek. It looks like someone must have once put a hatchet through his skull.

He grins at Ludwig in the rearview mirror. "Are you from Africa?"

"No. No, man, Philly. Philadelphia."

"Ah, yes, City of Brotherly Love, eh?"

"That's right. How'd you know that?"

"Everybody know that," the cabby says, grinning. "Everybody know. I, I come from Eritrea."

"Eritrea?"

"Yes. That is right. Do you know it? Do you know Eritrea?"

"No. No, I don't."

"It is a beautiful country, brother. But too much war. Too much. We have had civil war for many, many years. Almost all the time I was living there it was a war. Since I was a child even. That's why I leave. That's why I am here."

"I'm—I'm sorry about that," says Ludwig.

Out of an impulsive sense of kinship—for the man has clearly seen terrible things—and out of an inchoate guilt vaguely connected to the man's war-scarred past, Ludwig tips the cabby something extra and checks into the motel. When he reaches the room, he lies down and lets the air-conditioning blanket his body. When he wakes, it's half past noon. He showers and dresses. After, he watches news coverage of a suicide car bombing in Baghdad, with footage of the street, the ambulance, and the rubble, until he doesn't have it in him to watch another second. His eye falls on his rucksack. He turns off the TV and pulls out the envelope and the book Mrs. S. gave him. He pages through the book. It includes profiles of the different major arcana cards, summaries of the images on them, and their meanings. Soon he is immersed, reading about the different ways they can be read, the ways the readings can be interpreted. He thinks back to what Mrs. S. had said, about the possibility that a twenty-third card could hold some mysterious meaning—some kind of archetype. *What does that mean?* he wonders. *How could an image change anything?* He stares out the window, wishing that Mrs. S. had thought to include a deck of tarot cards with the book and the papers. After a while he closes the book and heads down to the lobby.

He finds a guest office with an old PC and prints a map of the Chatham address. The clerk at the desk tells him it's located in the Oakleigh Garden District, just west.

"It's a nice part of town," he says. "There's a lot of tourist attractions there. Historic landmarks. Here——" He goes to a panel of tourist pamphlets, grabs one, and gives it to Ludwig. "There's some stuff about the history in here."

"Thanks."

It doesn't take long to get to Chatham. The house is marked by a brass number on a high stone wall with two closed-circuit video cameras on both sides of a wrought-iron gate. The cameras ward him off. He passes in front of the house, but he keeps a safe distance across the street. He walks around the block to the backside of the property, where he sees that there are video cameras bolted to the trunks of some trees high off the ground on the other side of a wrought-iron service gate. Beyond it a driveway curves up and around some pine trees. But he can't see the house from the street. There's no way to get in, at least in daytime, without being seen.

A few blocks from his motel he finds a convenience store and buys two icy cold 40s of Olde English malt liquor and a prepaid cell phone. Back in the room, he lies down and drinks half a bottle too fast. He stares at the ceiling until he tumbles into a black whorl of terrifying dreams and memories.

They're taking fire, persistent, incredibly annoying fire that forces them to hunker down on the north side of a cratered stretch of Haifa Street in Baghdad. The windshield of the convoy's lead vehicle is blown out, but amazingly no one's badly hurt. They hold the position and wait the way they wait each and every day for something or other: fuel or food, flex-cuffs, armor or extra ammo, air support, an interpreter, some Big Guy from the Green Zone who wants to see The Situation. *Dawn. Dusk.*

And then after about an hour or two, whoever likely shot the Humvee in the first place opens up with withering fire, unusually accurate, that escalates into a bold barrage of rounds both light and heavy, booming out in a fan shape from a block of three- and four-story-high buildings. There are lots of balconies up there to hide on. Ludwig and the guys all take cover for a while, until it gets tedious. There's some confusion as to whether someone has already called in an air strike. Ludwig, hunkered down in the GPK on the Humvee, which is parked against a wall, has started to suspect that the day might get dull. But no air strike comes. The hawks are busy bombing someplace else. And then the lieutenant comes for Ludwig and his gun and tells him to put a cap up the asses of the guys shooting at them from the building down the way.

"He'll take 'em out, sir," says Ferrer. "Our guy's a wicked shot."

But Ludwig's not so sure. "Is it clear?" he says.

"It's a clear shot, all the way down the lane. Like a fucking bowling alley."

"I mean is it—"

"Just take the shot, Mason."

So they load on and drive up to the head of the line, where the road forms a terminal T and the walls of the houses on both sides of the intersection are all blown out and scattered.

Taking a shot from a place like that presents certain challenges. There are definitely snipers up there, Ludwig knows, men with sure aim. The second you're exposed—the second you fuck up and show yourself—you're the biggest, most desirable target of all because you're the Guy with the Gun. But above all, he's feeling kind of sick. He's used to a little more control, to the application of tried-and-true protocols. This, though, is all improv, seat-of-the-pants. He doesn't like it at all. When things are under his control, when all the protocols are followed—the t's all crossed and each i dotted, he customarily, perversely, at moments like those feels almost debonair. This is often the case when he's in dangerous situations. But he's always been that way, and he doesn't take it for courage. It isn't. It's about feeling alive, feeling adrenaline in his veins, feeling useful and purposeful, like the tip, the deadly point of a tremendous force, the thing that Vance calls the Will of Empire. It's a feeling so intense, it can make him forget for days the uncertainty and desperation that await him back home: Charlotte, alone there with their new kid with no help and a stack of bills to pay. His mother, her body irradiated yet still riddled with clots of metastasized cancer, buried in a graveyard in West Philly. No job prospects to speak of, or solid skills, unless being able to fire a .50 cal. from the top of a Humvee going sixty miles an hour is worth something to anyone outside of a war zone. But then, now, Ludwig's guts pulse with anxiety. He checks to make sure he has as much ammo on hand as possible. When Wonder, behind the wheel, reaches the corner, the lieutenant points toward what Ludwig should aim for: a tower, the minaret of a mosque, rising beyond and above the squat complex of low-rise buildings.

"The mosque? Back there?" Ludwig says.

"No, no, the tower above it," says the lieutenant. It's a crazy fast play on words and meaning. And it's pure bullshit, since the tower is the minaret, and the minaret marks the mosque. They are all one and the same. "Can't miss it. They're all in there. Almost all of 'em. Take down that fucking roach motel."

Ludwig, locked and loaded, swallows down the vomit in his throat and pops his knuckles. His eyes scan Ferrer's face, the lieutenant's, but they are all too far gone in the zone of their rage and fear, and their determination or resignation—he's not sure what it is—pulls him along like a tidal force. The second Wonder pulls the Humvee into position Ludwig opens fire down the way. When he sees movement on the balconies or in the window blocks in the mid-distance, he swings to it and fires until he doesn't see movement anymore. He takes fire too, hears it ping the Humvee hard and the p-p-p-ing-ing-p-p-ing against the gunner protection kit, the GPK, that shields the turret. Under him in the cab he hears Vance going Do it, man. Fuck'em. Yeah, man. Up left. Up left, his voice thick with adrenaline and murder. But Ludwig's only interested in seeing the chunks of concrete and dust fly off the tower. He wants to obliterate the tower, shatter it, bust it up so it'll tumble. After about five minutes he isn't getting the same kind of effect anymore. The upper half of the tower is a perforated, teetering calamity. Guys behind him are whooping and hollering, and Ludwig hears the command to stop and stops, just like that, checks that the gun's cooling okay, secures it, glances at the litter of spent casings strewn on the asphalt beside the Humvee.

Later, near dusk, they go toward what's left of the minaret. Powder, like fog, wafts and ebbs in the shadows and the evening light. They stagger over the concrete, the twisted rebar, the bent pipes and tangled wiring. The whole inside of the tower has collapsed. Rubble, glass, and tile spill out of the windows and doors. Parts of the walls have given way too. The engineers have told them to stay outside, so they skirt the devastation. The building lists a little. They come to a scene of surprising carnage. Unarmed men are running about, oblivious to the shouts to put their hands up, get down, hit the ground, making the marines nervous. Some guys are pointing their weapons at the men, but the men don't seem to care. More of them are sprinting out of alleyways, down streets, until a stampede is under way, a clamor of wild-eyed civilians climbing onto the heap of rubble that looks like it was once a one-story office building or storefront behind the minaret, now collapsed. The men pull free when marines try to hold them in place, plead, call out, claw at the dust, at the shattered cinder blocks. They scramble madly, wild-eyed. They could not care less about the threats, the raised weapons. They fall to their knees and dig.

Ludwig pushes his way through the line of marines encircling the chaos. "What is it? What's goin' on?" Ludwig asks Vance, who stands gazing on the ruins. Vance's eyes flare. He sets his hand on Ludwig's chest and pushes him urgently but gently backward. "You don't want to see this. Trust me, buddy."

"What is it?" Ludwig pushes back, but Vance is implacable. It's like pushing against a brick wall. Ludwig retreats two steps fast and outflanks him, rushes again toward to the rubble as Vance calls behind Stop him! Somebody get ahold of him! Don't let him—

Ludwig breaks through to the front edge of the crowd. What he sees does not make sense.

"What—What is this?" he says out loud.

Chessauri, a radioman, stares hollow eyed straight ahead. "Women," he says, as if to himself. "Kids. Some kinda nursery or somethin'."

Ludwig is astounded to see bodies everywhere. He'd long lived in fear that he would kill civilians and now he's done it. He sees their bodies half submerged in rubble and shards of glass, all powdered over with a delicate coat of concrete grit that settles thick and blue in the dusk light.

When he wakes, he bolts up straight, feeling nauseated and sick at heart. His shirt is soaked through. He sits at the edge of the bed and weeps, overwhelmed by the desolation in his heart. He rises, washes his face, stares out the window hoping for a meditative peace, but his thoughts turn dark and circle around the idea of an idea—the mystery of an unknown archetype. He lurches across the room for his pack and finds Mrs. S.'s phone number. It takes him a while to figure out how to use the cell phone. He leans against the wall as the phone rings.

"Hello?"

"Missus S.?"

"Ludwig?"

"Yeah. Sorry, Celia."

"It's okay. I'll get her."

He waits and thinks about hanging up. Why is he calling her? What does he expect to hear from her? He's out of it, he knows. He's a mess. She'll hear it in his voice, and she'll lose whatever misplaced confidence she has in him. He pulls the phone from his ear—

"Hello? Hello?"

He listens close. "Missus S."

"Ludwig? Is that you?"

"Yeah."

"I got your message from the other day. How are you? Do you need something?"

"Yeah. Listen. Can I ask you something? I gotta ask you something."

"Are you okay? You sound strange. What is it?"

"Those cards. The tarot cards. They all have pictures on them. You said your deck has twenty-three of these cards. All the cards have meanings, right? The pictures. The—the archetypes? Right? You must've thought a lot about what the picture on that twenty-third card might be. What do you think it is?"

"I already told you. I really don't know."

"Well, what *do* you know?"

"It's difficult to explain. The cards have very specific and complex meanings. You have to—"

"Just tell me!" It comes out louder and harsher than he intended and he suspects it has a lot to do with the drinking and the residue of oxy in his system—her oxy. But after that dream, after all the nightmarish memories that threaten to crowd out his sanity, he's overcome by the desire to know. It's as if the answers to everything—the reason for the terrible mayhem that day at the mosque, the reason his friends got killed, the reason he saw the black sun, and the reason he has had to grapple through all the bleak days since the Box—it's as if all of it might be held in the deck, in the missing card. There must be a reason that *he* survived that day, that *he* was sent to Landstuhl, that *he* met Sonia, and that she called *him* to do this—this crazy thing. Maybe there is something to this deck.

"I'm sorry," he says. "I just—I need to know. I need to know what you know."

"Ah. Well, of course. Are you—? You sound so strange."

Ludwig hesitates. "Just, please, tell me," he says.

"Okay. I'll try. I don't know, but I have this—this idea. I looked for years at the known deck, the major arcana and all the pips and cups and sword cards, too, and I tried to guess at what's missing.

What archetype could be missing? What part of us—our *humanity*, our human *experience*—might be missing? It's like a kind of calculus, but instead of numbers you have symbols, the symbols that give our lives meaning. But what if the set of symbols is incomplete? You have to think, what more are we? What could be missing? What have we not considered? Is there something about who we are that we haven't considered? Who we can be?"

"What *do* you think it could be?"

"I *don't know*, Ludwig. I wish I knew. I wish I could remember. I sometimes wonder if it's something so obvious, we take it for granted. Maybe the card in my mother's deck is a symbol of evil, an archetype of war, of violence. I've hoped for years, though, that it's a symbol of some kind of new consciousness, of love, not romantic love, but the love that helps us feel empathy, compassion. But in the end, I just—don't know."

Ludwig shuts his eyes. He had wanted certainty, but now he understands that he would never have it. "Okay," he says. "I guess I—get it."

"Do you? Do you really?"

"The other day you said I probably know something about the kinds of things you've seen. What did you mean by that?"

She's silent for a moment. "I know from things that Sonia has said that the situation there, in the place you call the Box, is very tough, very ugly. It's hard, maybe impossible, for people who haven't seen it to understand. I know that Sonia has been having a difficult time since she returned. I know that feeling. I assumed that you know that feeling too."

Ludwig stares out the window and blanks. Beyond the sprawling parking lot and the trees and hedges bordering it, he sees the traffic pass in the bright, hot afternoon. He finds that tears are running down his face, but he doesn't know exactly why.

"You know—I'm married?" he says.

"You told me. You have a son."

"Yeah. That's right." Ludwig closes his eyes. "It's been so fucked up. Sorry. I shouldn't—"

"It's okay, Ludwig. It's okay."

He opens his eyes. "I see stuff from the Box all the time."

"It's hard to forget. I don't want to say impossible, but I have to be honest. The war ended sixty years ago and I still see things as if they happened yesterday."

"But it's not just that—I see those things. The things that happened, but I also see things that—haven't happened." He squints at the shimmering leaves of the trees, the bright skyline. Cars curve along a distant overpass. "I see myself hurting my family, my wife. I—I can't help it."

"Oh, Ludwig. I'm so sorry." There is a long silence and then she speaks. "I'm so sorry for you, for Sonia, for all of you who have had to see these things."

He can hear from her voice that she's weeping. Ludwig wipes his eyes and face with his fingers. "Does it really matter? Finding this thing?"

"I don't know. Maybe not. It's just—something that I've thought a lot about."

"I'll find it."

"Yes. Please. Thank you, Ludwig. I shouldn't be so hopeful, but I am. Please find it."

"Bye, Missus S."

"Goodbye, Ludwig."

He stands and staggers and leans against the window frame. She had said that symbols give our lives meaning. He guesses that he knows what she means, but as he stares out at the parking lot he dwells on the part about our lives, the thing itself, the living part, the flesh and blood, like Sam and Charlotte.

In his room, after a long afternoon of aimless wandering, after making brief stops in a bookstore to buy a box of tarot cards and a nearby sports equipment store to buy some clothes, and after chasing a late dinner of a cheeseburger and onion rings with a Coke, he dresses as if for a jog: black sweatpants, black T-shirt, and a black hooded sweatshirt.

He isn't so sure how safe it is for a black guy to go jogging late at night this far south of the Mason-Dixon, but by midnight he gets there, back to the Garden District, back to the Chatham Street house. On the last few blocks he cinches his hood nearly shut and jogs straight to the house, darts across the quiet street that runs along the rear, and vaults up one of the stone posts beside the back gate. Up top he perches for a moment to get his bearings before he drops between the wall and the stands of pine that line it. He climbs out and brushes himself off.

Up the path, treading slow, the place is just so still, so quiet. Ahead he spies a door with a small portico flanked on each side by a line of waist-high bushes under banks of French doors. He eyes the asphalt path, sees no lights at all, only the moonlight. He walks to one of the French doors near the corner of the house, peeks inside, scans an empty room. There's no furniture, nothing on the walls. Just an expanse of wood floor that leads from that large and empty room into what looks like another large and empty room. He balls his hand into the sleeve of his sweatshirt and punches out a window frame, waits, listens. He hears no alarm, no sound, no movement. How can this be? He opens the door and enters. He walks fast to the next room, and the next. No furniture. In the foyer, on a table against the wall, he sees real estate listing sheets, a stack of a local agent's business cards. He goes to the kitchen and catches glints of light on chrome fixtures, silver marble, the floor beside the door. He kneels, finds shards of broken glass. He looks at the door, pushes aside the shade, sees the shattered pane, the dead bolt below it. On the island in the middle of the kitchen he sees a pair of wraparound shades. He folds them closed, puts them in his sweatpants pocket. He crosses to a curved stairway, climbs up, walks the length of the hall, and scans the empty rooms. Red and blue lights flash against the wall in a room whose high windows overlook the front yard. Ludwig bounds down the stairs to the foyer, around to the room he first entered, looks back. He sees the lights across the hall. The car is out front. He steps out through the French door, pads around the hedges. He hears a voice, maybe a radio from the side to his left. He steps to the path and he hears something, a fast-approaching *jingle jingle* like car keys flying through the air. Then he sees it: a dog, a black dog, a lanky, fast-running dog bolting toward him down the path. Ludwig darts toward the stone wall.

Running, running fast around the curve. Rapid-fire padfalls come up fast behind him. Up ahead, only the silhouettes of pine trees. He sees no wall, no trellis, no standpipe, nothing to climb. The dog is getting closer and there's no getting away. He isn't going to make it. No options. Nothing. Yes. Maybe one. He feints fast toward his left, his right. He hears the dog grunt. He runs for the trees to his right and crashes through the low branches, shields his face with his upheld arms. The dog darts through the brush. Loping, growling, tentative starts behind Ludwig as he rushes through the underbrush and branches, looks for the wall, the wall, any hint of the wall. Finally he slams into it with his forearm. He takes a step back, leaps up, grabs ahold of the edge. The dog gets his left boot. It growls, twists frenziedly, back and forth, back and forth. Its whole weight is on his leg. Ludwig kicks, climbs, kicks again but it won't let go. He claws at the wall, kicks back, scrambles up. Halfway over the wall he kicks again and the dog lets go with a humiliated whine. It barks and leaps and circles in the brush under him. *Fucker*, Ludwig hisses.

Safe on the sidewalk, he looks up and down the street. A car idles half a block away. Was it there before? He crouches, squints, thinks he sees the silhouette of someone in the driver's seat, but he hears voices now, men on the other side of the wall. He steps off the curb, and the car engine guns. He stops, looks up. The headlights flare and he holds his forearm up to shield his eyes. He hesitates, takes another step. The car charges at him. He dodges left, right, the car shoots toward him. He leaps for the curb. The car runs up the concrete. *Hey*, he yells. The passenger side-view mirror catches his forearm. The car swerves to a stop half a block away. It stands driver side to Ludwig. He stares at it, breathless, spots a stock-still figure at the wheel. He's paralyzed, caught between his fear of the car and of the voices rising on the other side of the wall. A man calls out. The dog barks. The car stands still in the road. Ludwig backs away, turns and runs.

Back at the motel, sacked out on the bed, nursing the bruise on his arm with a bagful of ice and floating easy on the current of half a pint of J&B, Ludwig punches the channel up button until he reaches the nosebleed heights, the double digits reserved for marketers of miracle juicers, kitchen knives as sharp as diamond cutters, salad spinners, and endless varieties of diet pills and energy drinks. He settles on a channel with old cartoons, and as he stares at the screen he dwells on the things that Mrs. S. had said the day before and his own confession, about the dreams that haunt him. But the thought of those dreams provoke his anxiety, and his eyes dart to his rucksack, which holds the vial of oxy. But he sticks to the whiskey and focuses on the money, on what the money can buy, what it can help him do. He dwells on that until he passes out.

———

Vance wakes him with a gentle kick to the sole of his boot.

"Yo, Lud, bud. Wake up, man. It's time to go."

Ludwig sits up on the edge of his cot. The others rise. Soon they're geared up and all on board and they're on the road again, patrolling. Vance is at the wheel. Tops on Lieutenant LaMantia's list, their current priority: an operative, a suspected hajji named Jawad Attiya in Tikrit. The location is in a neighborhood of shops just west of where they now drive. Most of the storefronts are dark. Dusk gives way to night, a rising anxiety. The evening smells of jasmine and diesel and garbage. The three Humvees stop at the address, a corner shop. Lieutenant LaMantia calls for six men. They all know who they are and Ludwig is one of them. The lieutenant knocks. Two women answer.

No, they say. The man in the photo is not known to them.

Can we take a look inside? Do you mind if we take a moment of your time to check?

A moment of your time, thinks Ludwig. Ha. A back-and-forth ensues. It's always the same. Until finally they relent because maybe they understand as Ludwig and the others understand that if they have come all this way—all the way from Am-e-ree-ka—that it's likely they have nothing better to do than insist and insist and insist far into the night. And so they go inside. Through the tidy shop, up stairs so narrow and a ceiling so low, he can barely climb with his weapon and his night goggles and his gear. Burd stays in the store. Ferrer stays at the bottom of the stairs. At the top is a small apartment redolent of food, of onions and beef. Ornate, carved chairs upholstered in crimson and aqua. Two sofas frame an entertainment center lined with family photos arrayed around a big-screen TV. And two girls stand in a doorway. Solomon and Blom go straight for the family photos and study them one by one with flashlights.

But where is Jawad? asks Lieutenant LaMantia. He lives here. We know he lives here. People see him come and go from here.

No, no, they say. Who says this? We do not know this boy although this boy looks very much like the boy who takes our garbage in the evenings.

Sean. Sean, help me out, says Lieutenant LaMantia.

Yessir.

Can you talk to this lady here while I talk to her daughter?

Yessir. Can you stand over here? Right here? I just need a moment of your time. Your daughter says the boy takes out the garbage? What's the boy's name?

And the lieutenant and Driscoll play out the well-practiced game. It's not so much good-cop, bad-cop as divide and conquer. Tease out the inconsistencies, the misaligned facts and statements. Separate the mother and the daughter so that they stress and break under the pressure of incriminating either each other or themselves. On it goes.

Ludwig stands at the top of the stairs, holding his gun. That's his job. He watches for quick movements in the doors, unexpected action. In the bedroom, behind the girls, he spies Solomon and Blom scour over a dresser lined with bottles, a tall metal file cabinet. He looks down and hesitates under the relent-less gaze of the taller girl. She has on a black hijab. Why is she looking at him that way? He smiles, but she doesn't blink. She doesn't smile. She's unmoved. He starts to sweat. His mouth grows dry. He strokes the trigger of his gun. She's slender, a stick, like a boy. Her eyes are big and black as sleep. Why is she staring at him? Why is she looking at him that way?

———————

When he wakes up, it's nearly ten, but there's a shadow, like a storm, in the distance to the south. He feels wired, feels course through him the thrill of past adrenaline and heat, the humidity, the strangeness of it all. The sense of mission rushes through his veins. He has always preferred intensity to its opposite. He does not do so well when things are not extreme. He does not perform well in inertia.

But the rush he'd felt earlier turns to lethargy. To ward it off, he starts to pack his things. He stuffs his toothbrush and razor, the tarot book and the envelope in his rucksack. As he balls up his new sweat-pants he feels the sunglasses in the pocket and pulls them out. Shiny black lenses and beige ballistic frames. They look expensive. They're familiar from his days in the Box. He peers at the small lettering on the inside of the left temple: *For Ghebelin Security Enterprises*. And on the right temple: *For Ghebelin Security Enterprises*.

He turns the glasses over in his hands. He thinks back to the night: the house, the cameras, the broken glass, the dog, the car that nearly ran him over. Ghebelin Security. He goes to the wastebasket beside the dresser, reaches in, pulls out the pamphlet the motel clerk gave him, and flattens it out: *The Oakleigh Garden District*. He opens it up. Inside are some photos of big houses, a drawing of an old mansion, a few paragraphs about the history of the area, suggestions for a self-guided tour beside a small map labeled with arrows. He turns it over. On the last panel is a list of trustees, benefactors, and sponsors who've supported efforts to preserve the district. His gaze scrolls down and snags on a line: *Commander Hugo Ghebelin, in loving memory of Christine and Stephan Ghebelin, beloved mother and father*.

On the computer in the motel guest office he types in Hugo Ghebelin's name. The first hits that come up are all about things he already knows. Ghebelin Security Enterprises, or GSE, headed by Hugo Ghebelin, runs private security in Iraq, Kuwait, UAE, and Afghanistan, including protective services for the State Department and Department of Defense, bodyguard and convoy security for diplomats, senators and other VIPs from Washington, and visiting officers from Central Command.

Ludwig types in Ghebelin's name and adds Mobile, Alabama. Some of the Oakleigh Garden District stuff comes up. And here, just as he hoped, some history:

Hugo Ghebelin's great-grandfather, Théophile Ghebelin, a steel magnate, made his fortune in the Mobile area building drydocks, funded by federal loans at the turn of the century. Later, he'd moved farther west, to New Orleans, and started work for the New York

Shipbuilding Corporation building dreadnoughts and steel armor for the US Navy. Around that time he'd married a woman of note there, in New Orleans, a mulatta, Haitian, named Marquise Ghebelin, who practiced voodoo and fortune-telling. Between 1909 and 1912 they built a mansion that became known as *La Marquise*. It still stands somewhere in New Orleans, an architecturally significant but little-known holding of the Louisiana Trust for Historic Preservation.

Generations of Ghebelins built on the foundation lain by Théophile. His son expanded the company aggressively from the 1920s to the Korean War. His grandson, Stephan, grew the secretive but influential firm even more during the conflict in Vietnam and in the last decades of the Cold War. And his great grandson, Hugo, has stewarded the company into the 21st century and the War on Terror. Ghebelin Inc. is now the country's foremost military and security contractor.

Ludwig's stomach starts to growl. He looks at the photos of Hugo Ghebelin in Baghdad, in Kabul, as a Navy SEAL in Panama in '89, giving testimony to a US Senate panel in the lead-up to the invasion of Iraq, standing in the middle of a cluster of robed sheikhs beside a desert landing strip somewhere in Kuwait. Ludwig pauses at a photo of Ghebelin from the early nineties, around the time he'd fought in Desert Storm, wearing dress blues and a white lid. He's a handsome, kind of generic-looking white guy with jet-black hair, a stiff smile, and stone-gray eyes. Ludwig's struck by the fact that although Ghebelin's name seemed to be written on the side of half the pickup trucks and 4Runners in the Box, he's never actually *seen* any pictures of him, until now.

He turns off the computer and sees his own face reflected in the screen. *New Orleans*, he thinks. "What've you got to lose?" he mutters.

He packs his things and goes downstairs to check out. The woman at the counter gives him his receipt.

"Did you find your friend?"

"What?"

"Your friend. Your family friend. He said you were—" She frowns, as if she's starting to doubt herself, then cocks her head. "Did someone call you in your room? Earlier? A man?"

"No."

Her eyes widen. "Ooh."

"Why?" he asks. "What is it?"

"Well, there *was* a man, earlier. But maybe he was— Maybe he thought you were somebody else?"

"Here? Someone came here? To see me?"

She covers her face. "Oh God. I might have misunderstood who he was looking for."

"It's no big deal," says Ludwig.

He takes the receipt and heads out. It's hot. He sets out for a diner, thinking about a bite to eat, some eggs, maybe bacon, and definitely coffee. A couple blocks down, a car slows at the curb beside him.

"Yo, buddy," someone says. "Yo, Ludwig, over here."

Ludwig looks at the car. There's a man, an old white guy, driving slow along the curb in a blue Nissan Maxima pointing a gun at him through the open passenger-side window. Ludwig stops. The car stops. He's pretty sure it's the same car that almost ran him over the night before. Ludwig looks to his right, to his left, and back at the car. The man leans across, pushes open the door, and hitches the gun at him.

"Yo, kid, get in the fucking car or I'll shoot you."

It's a Smith & Wesson, a .38 Special, the same kind of gun Ludwig's dad used to keep in a box under his bed. The same kind of gun he shot himself with. Ludwig climbs into the car. The man throws the rucksack into the backseat of the car and pushes Ludwig hard against the dashboard.

"Don't try anything," the man says. He reaches around and pulls Ludwig's arms behind him. Ludwig feels the cold metal of handcuffs, twists his arms, but the stranger has the cuffs locked fast. The man pulls him back and Ludwig pushes his arms to his right to get his elbows out of the way so he can lean back. The car bolts away from the curb. Ludwig glances sidelong but both of the man's hands are on the steering wheel. Where did the gun go? Where did he put it?

"Don't move," the man says.

"All right. All right," says Ludwig. "I'm not goin' anywhere."

The man is wearing black pants, a dark gray windbreaker, a black baseball cap, and sunglasses. He drives fast down quiet streets, pulls onto a ramp, and merges onto a highway. The heat is stifling.

"Can you open the window?"

The man switches on the AC. It rasps and shoots hot air into their faces. "It'll cool down in a second," he says.

They head west, judging by the sun. Ludwig doesn't want to look directly at the man. He doesn't want to spook him. But between his first sighting and a few furtive side-glances, he knows that something's off. The man has some kind of scar or burn running down part of his face.

"Where're we headed?" Ludwig asks.

The man doesn't answer. He stares at the road ahead. He drives slow and hogs the center lane. Faster traffic, going sixty and above, careens out from behind to pass. A woman on the right glares at them as she cruises past. The man takes an exit ramp onto a service road that runs alongside clusters of mobile homes and row upon row of squat, square bungalows. After a while it all peters out to an eerie wasteland of abandoned factories and shuttered warehouses.

The air conditioner starts to run okay. Cool air strokes Ludwig's face. The man flicks on the radio. Pop jingles out. He turns the dial fast: jazz, talk radio, pop, classical, more pop. "Shit," he says. He flicks it off.

About thirty minutes into the ride, Ludwig has lost all sensation in his arms. He sees a row of corrugated metal buildings surrounded by high metal fences and weed-choked blacktop. Such desolation. He eyes it all as they ride past, searches without success for signs, addresses, any clue to tell where he is.

The man takes a turn and drives to a dead end bordered by a palisade of tar-coated posts. Tall grass waves in the breeze atop a sand berm beyond the posts, and seagulls rise and dip above. They've come to the coast. The man turns, which gives Ludwig his first chance to look at what he's dealing with. A burn scars the right side of the man's face and most of his forehead. Sunglasses hide his eyes.

"Jesus," says Ludwig.

"Whatsa matter? Not feelin' the love? Listen, we're gonna get out here. Don't do anything stupid. You try and move or you yell or anything like that I'll shoot you in the face. You understand?"

Ludwig gets out of the car. He thinks about running but he's sure the man's good for his word.

"Lean up against the car. Spread your legs."

Ludwig faces the car. The man pushes him forward, kicks the insides of his ankles, and rifles through his pockets. He pulls out his cell phone, pats down his ankles, his waist, and under his arms. He holds Ludwig's wrists close and unlocks the handcuffs.

"Okay. Stand up."

Ludwig stands up.

"You try and run I'll shoot you in the back. Doesn't matter how fast you think you can run, I'll put a fucking bullet through your spine."

"All right."

The man shoves him and Ludwig stumbles toward the palisade. When they reach it, the man presses the gun into Ludwig's back.

"Go on."

Ludwig clamors over the wood posts. The man comes after him. Ludwig pushes his fingers into the sand to climb the steep berm. He thinks of taking a fistful and flinging it into the man's face but then he thinks of the sunglasses and decides against it. At the top of the hill he finds himself in a thicket of tall, sharp grass.

"Keep walking," says the man.

Ludwig walks under the diving gulls and the bright blue sky. He comes to a clearing. Gulls burst from a mudflat. Flies follow, buzzing in a sudden frenzy. Fish carcasses litter the moist dirt around a few rusted oil barrels. Rows of barrels and stacks of tires encircle a small black shack. The place smells like salt and rotting fish and decaying rubber. The Gulf must be just beyond the grass across the clearing, he thinks. Or is it, as he'd just discovered, a bay?

The man stands with the gun pointed at him and holds a small black duffel bag in his other hand. "Get down. Sit down right there. Right over there."

Ludwig sits on an overturned barrel. He's finely tuned to the world. He feels the fuel that makes it go round running through the surging valves of his heart. He's keen on sounds, the smell of death and rot. The air feels sharp and hot, but sharpest and hottest of all is a feeling of longing and regret. Charlotte and Sam, he thinks, will never know that he died here.

"What are you doing?" he says.

The man moves his arm fast and Ludwig feels it in his right knee, hard as a hammer blow. He gasps and grabs hold of his leg. "Motherfucker."

The man steps back and sits on an upturned barrel a few feet away. He sets the duffel bag at his feet and takes off his baseball cap. A crude comb-over fails to conceal the burns on his head. He sets his cap on his lap, gazes up at the sky, and presses errant wisps of gray hair against his scalp. "*Luuu*dwig Mason," he murmurs. "Lud*wiiiig* Mason. Ludwig *Maaa*son. Ludwig—"

"Who are you? What the fuck are you doing?"

The man looks down. "What'm *I* doing?"

Ludwig sees himself: tiny, seated, pathetic, reflected in the mirrored sunglasses.

"You should ask yourself what *you're* doing. Ask yourself that. I saw you outside the Ghebelin house yesterday and then again last night. He sent you. He knows I'm coming for him so he sent you to find me. To stop me."

"*What?* What're you talkin' about?"

The man points the gun at him. "Don't mess with me, kid. Don't waste my fucking time 'cause I don't have much. I know what you're up to."

Ludwig hesitates. "I don't know what you're talking about." The sunglasses stare at him. Ludwig takes a deep breath and looks across the stretch of seaside desolation, a killing field for seagulls. *What a place to die*, he thinks. He turns back, eyes the gun, looks up. "This is some kind of mistake. I'm not who you think I am."

The burned man nods. "I know who you are. You're Marine Corporal Ludwig Mason. Third Battalion, Fifth Marines. Back from Iraq just last December. I made some calls. Talked to some old buddies."

He sits quiet for a while. Ludwig grows tense. Then, "What was it like for you there?"

"There?"

"Iraq."

Ludwig takes a deep breath. "It's war."

The burned man nods thoughtfully. His sunglasses gaze off toward the horizon. "You know, I gotta say, I feel sorry for you guys. I really do. When we came back from Nam, people fucking *hated* us. They screamed at us, spat on us. It must be real weird going through all that and then coming back to"—the man shakes his head, shrugs—"nothin'."

"What service were you in?"

"Huh." The man smiles. "Rootin' around, huh? Don't bother. You can see me, but I'm not here. Listen. Enough. Go home. There's nothing to see here. If your boss asks you what happened, just tell him you did the deed, get your pay. By the time he figures out you lied I'll get to him." The man pauses. "Or, just tell him the damn truth. Tell him I'm coming for him." His jaw twists into a grim smile. "Wonder how he'd handle that."

Ludwig stares. "I don't—work for whoever it is you're talking about."

"C'mon now. Don't play tough. Why would you risk anything for these people?" He shakes his head, roots through the inside pocket of his jacket with his free hand, stands, and walks the few paces toward Ludwig until he's standing over him. He pulls out a toothpick and sets at his teeth with it. "Tell me." He flicks the toothpick away and points the gun at Ludwig's forehead. "Where's Ghebelin?"

"Please God. If I knew, I'd— Listen. Please. I've got a son, a little boy."

"You know what? I have a kid, too, somewhere. Far as he knows, I've been dead for fifteen years." He cocks the gun. "They're young and flexible. They get used to being fatherless."

More for shame than self-protection, Ludwig shields his eyes with his hand. He feels his lungs give out, a kind of free fall in his chest that takes his whole heart with him. Seagulls hover and plummet in the wind. Where are Charlotte and Sam at that very moment? He waits.

"Hey," the burned man says. "Where'd you get that tattoo?"

Ludwig hears a sound behind him and swivels toward the shack. A kid, a black boy in jeans and a yellow T-shirt and blue rain boots, with a fishing pole in one hand and a yellow tackle box in the other, stands staring at them.

Ludwig looks at the burned man, and the burned man looks at him. Ludwig turns back to the kid. "Run!" he shouts.

The burned man shakes his head and wipes his mouth. "Fuck." He kneels and unzips the duffel bag. "Don't fucking move or I *will* kill you." He draws out a sawed-off shotgun, rises, rushes forward, and swings the stock into the side of Ludwig's head. Ludwig rolls to the dirt. When the fire in his head flares out, he kneels and rises. The pole and the tackle box lie in the mud. The boy has vanished. The burned man pumps the shotgun and takes a step toward the spot where the boy had been standing.

Ludwig rises. "Run," he yells again. "Don't stop. He'll k—" The shotgun stock slams into his face again.

When he opens his eyes, he sees no one in the clearing, no movement. He touches his cheek, looks up when he hears the man call out to stop, and jolts at the sound of a shout and a shot. He rises and runs into the channel of trampled grass, runs toward the sound. As he gets closer he slows. To the left and right no sign of anyone so far as he can see. But he hears the sound of someone running. He goes in that direction. After a while he can't hear anything. He stops and crouches. Half a minute passes, maybe another. He hears the grass move and he stops breathing. The grass whispers to his right; the sound rises. He poises to rush the man, but the sound stops. He waits, rises, pads toward the source of the sound. The sound of breathing stops as he parts the grass. The boy stares at him. Thin, hair close-cropped, a straight dark scar across his left cheek. His face is coated with sweat, and his eyes are wide and terrified. Ludwig puts his finger to his lips. They wait. A sound rises from Ludwig's left. He gestures to the boy to crouch. The crackle of falling grass rises. The boy stares at him, shaking. Ludwig struggles to control his own breathing. The sound rises. Ludwig gestures to the boy to stay still. Then he rises slowly. The sound stops. Ludwig steps slowly away from the boy. The rustling stalks him. The boy's eyes go wider. He stares at him, stricken. He thinks that Ludwig is abandoning him. Ludwig puts his finger to his lips again. He takes another step backward. The stalks break crisply under his boot. The rustling rushes him. Ludwig turns and runs. As he pushes through the grass he hears the man coming after him. He runs across the clearing and into the grass again. He climbs the berm and tumbles down and vaults over the palisade. The driver-side window of the burned man's car is open. He reaches in, grabs his rucksack, turns and looks at the long road between the warehouses, looks back up at the berm. *He's coming*, he thinks. *He's coming.* He runs.

11.

He scales a fence a quarter mile up the road and runs around the side of a shuttered warehouse. He crouches and waits. Soon enough the man's car passes, cruising slow. Ludwig watches the car bear north on the access road. He goes to the edge of the lot and waits for another quarter hour, but he doesn't see anything. When he gets to the clearing, he stops. The fishing pole and the tackle box lie in the mud. He runs into the grass, weaves his way through the trampled grass, but he finds no trace of the boy. Save for the abandoned gear, he may as well have been a figment of a dream. He goes back to the road and sets out. When he reaches the highway, he watches the traffic with a mix of hope and dread.

About two miles up the road he sees a shopping plaza and darts into a SaveRight. As soon as he walks through the sliding doors his skin turns to ice. He's terrified, scared shitless, his mind jabbering with fear. He's afraid the man will jump out and shoot him in the face. He threads back and forth along the aisles senselessly until he finds the men's room, where he throws cold water on his face and ducks into a stall. Perched on the toilet seat, he pops an oxycodone and listens to the white noise shoot from the vent above, listens for the door or any voice. He starts to suspect that the man hasn't tracked him, but he needs to be sure. He goes back into the hall outside the restroom and dials 9-1-1 on the pay phone.

"Emergency service, how can I help you?"

"I wanna report a shooting."

"A shooting? Did somebody get shot?"

"I don't know. It just happened. It just happened about an hour ago."

"Where are you located, sir?"

"It happened outside Mobile, in Alabama. Near the Brookley Field Airport. It's somewhere south—"

"I need *your* location. I need to know where you are."

"I'm calling from a pay phone. You—You know exactly where I am."

"You said this happened just now?"

"Yes. Yes, just south of Mobile. Near Brookley Airport. Is that right? Or is it the Mobile Regional Aiport?"

"Sir. Sir. I need you to listen. Are you reporting a homicide, sir? Were you involved in a homicide? Or did you witne—"

"Just fucking listen, okay? There's a crazy motherfucker out here somewhere. He's got a scar or a burn on half his head. He's driving a blue Nissan Maxima, Alabama license plate number 5T7 BVB, and he just tried to kill me and a kid just south of Mobile, near the Brookley Airport or Complex. He shot at us. I think it's a rental car. Someone should check near the airport. It's like twenty minutes south of—"

"Sir, sir. I need more information. I need to know where you're loc—"

Ludwig hangs up. He waits one minute, dials zero.

"Operator, I've got an emergency. We need help."

"What's the problem, sir?"

"There's a robbery here. There's a man with a shotgun."

"The man has a shotgun?"

"Yes. Yes. He's armed."

"Are you calling from a pay phone?"

"That's right."

"Can you confirm the address? Where are you located?"

"I don't know the address. I'm at the SaveRight. The SaveRight, on the highway? Outside of Mobile? I think it's one-six-three? Or maybe it's Dauphin? Outside of Mobile? South of—"

"The Dauphin Island Parkway?"

"That's it! That's right. Please God, send help fast. He's crazy. He's waving the shotgun around. We need help."

"Is anybody hurt? Hello? Is any—"

Ludwig hangs up and looks at his watch. He waits for the sound of sirens and heads to the front of the store, where he spots two police cruisers out in the parking lot and two officers talking with a woman at the customer service counter. Another cop is headed toward the back of the store, but he doesn't look too rushed. It doesn't matter. Ludwig hopes that if the man is nearby, the cops and their cruisers will ward him off. Meantime, he browses. The aisles start to blur, but he's not sure what part is panic and what part is the oxy. He tries to stay steady and walk straight, goes through the motions of shopping until, after a while, he finds throughout the store a comforting uniformity of color, of lighting, of sound and atmosphere, and he discovers with a great feeling of relief that the SaveRight is just like the SaveRight he used to work at in Philly and like every other SaveRight he's ever been in since he was a kid. As chaotic as everything is, it amazes him how familiar the store feels. So he fleet-foots it past the watches and jewelry section, past the cosmetics and greeting cards, past the women's apparel and shoes to the two-aisle-wide snack foods section. After he buys a bottle of water, two Snickers bars, a bag of gummy bears, and a jar of salted peanuts, he heads to the entrance and wolfs down half the jar of peanuts. Then he finds a spot near the rows of shopping carts and stares into the blue afternoon. He watches the traffic come and go with a keen eye out for the burned man's car.

Fifteen minutes later he asks the lady at customer service if he can call or have them call for a cab. They call a cab for him, and while he waits he buys a cell phone and a calling card. When the cab comes, he hops in and tells the driver to take him to downtown Mobile.

———

In an alley downtown around the corner from his motel he leans up against a wall and closes his eyes until the world stops spinning. He pulls out the cell phone and fumbles as he searches for Mrs. S.'s number in his wallet. Celia answers.

"It's Ludwig."

"I'll get Missus S."

Mrs. S. gets on the line. "Yes, hello. Ludwig?"

"This thing's going bad."

"What? What's going on?"

"There's a crazy guy here. I think he's looking for the deck, or at least he's looking for the people who have the deck. He's following me. He's got a shotgun, and he nearly killed me and a kid near the airport."

"*What?* What kid?"

"I don't know. Just some—some kid, near the highway."

"My God. What happened?"

"I called the police. I'm gonna see if there's any way to get the police."

"My God. You have to stop all of this. You have to get out of there. This has gone too far. Someone's clearly gone insane. If—"

"Listen. Listen to me. I can handle this."

"*Handle* this? Handle *what*? No. No. Get out of there. It's starting to get—"

A van comes up the alleyway. Ludwig holds the phone to his chest and steps to the side to let it pass. When he pulls his palm off the phone, Mrs. S.'s voice leaps out.

"Ludwig! Ludwig!"

"I'm here. I'm here."

"Where did you go?"

"I'm on the street here."

"You sound so strange. This is a nightmare. You'll come home, then?"

He looks up the alley. "Listen, does the name Ghebelin mean anything to you?"

"Ghebelin?"

"Yeah. Yeah. You know it?"

"Of course, the Ghebelins are in that book I gave you. Haven't you read it?"

"Ah." He closes his eyes, leans against the wall, and thinks back to all the books he should have read, the high school assignments he should have done but didn't, way back in the day. He's jonesing hard. Bursts of color—red, yellow—explode in his mind. He sees the boy crouching in the grass. He wants to sit down.

"Ludwig? Ludwig, are you there? Will you come back?"

He opens his eyes. "I don't know," he says.

"What? But you have to!"

"I gotta go."

"Ludwig, please. Please. Stop now. I'll pay you. I'll give you money. Anything you need. You've already gone so far."

"I'll call you if I need anything. Bye, Missus S."

"Ludwig! Lud—"

He hangs up.

He finds a diner a few blocks away and wolfs down a plate of scrambled eggs and sausage. After, feeling sick, he goes to the men's room and dry heaves but he can't throw up. He heads to the train station and checks the schedules. The next train is slated to leave for New Orleans at half past eight. He buys a one-way ticket, lugs his rucksack to a bank of chairs, and sits in an anxious cold sweat.

With four hours to wait, his mind starts to wander. He wants to pop another oxy, but he fights it. There's too much of it in him mixed with adrenaline, and now his mind is no longer his. But the pills in the vial tucked in his pack shout for his attention, their pleas are muffled only a little by the child-safety cap. He must admit that though he's terrified, he's also buzzed. What scares him most is himself and the purgatory of days without purpose or mission. He stares at people. A little kid darts back and forth between the vending machines. His mother sits with a baby on her lap, reading a magazine. An old man in a powder-blue three-piece suit sits reading a paper a few chairs away. The place feels abandoned, too quiet. Ludwig can't sit still. So he crosses to the Mr. Dog on the far side of the parking lot. When the waitress comes by he orders a Coke. A football game is playing on the TV behind the cash register.

He closes his eyes, tries to shut the world out, but the chanting pills and the couple sitting at the table next to him distract him. Ludwig glances over. His eye catches a tattooed number thirty-seven under an upheld fist brandishing a dagger under the edge of the man's T-shirt sleeve. Ludwig studies the guy. He looks Hispanic. He has a crew cut and a grin so bright and full of confidence, Ludwig wonders if he's some kind of sociopath. The girl seated across from the guy is beautiful. She's black, maybe half-Hispanic. Her curly hair is bundled in a yellow headscarf, and when at one point she leans back in laughter at something the man says, Ludwig sees that she is pregnant.

"You tired?" the guy asks the girl.

"I'm all right." Her voice sounds like a kid's.

"We'll get some food."

"Oh, is *that* why we came in here?"

The guy smiles and touches the girl's hair and they whisper to each other. They remind Ludwig of the way he and Charlotte used to be together. The world had once been theirs. The guy looks up at Ludwig and Ludwig looks away. His heart swings wild loops inside his chest. He can't get the shotgun blast out of his head, the look of terror in that boy's eyes. He cringes, mortified by how far off he's wandered from a sane and steady path.

He turns his right palm downward and stares at the intaglioed welts, the silver and gray and slate rays that shoot from the dense black core of the tattoo sun. When did it all start to go so wrong? Was it when he signed up? Was it when he landed in the Box? Or was it sometime later, maybe over the last months back home? During all the days and weeks floating in a zoned-out stupor while Charlotte bore all the weight of their responsibilities and all the burden of their anxieties? Maybe it was when he hung up the phone and let Sonia's voice linger in his thoughts? Let the memory of her seduce him into this nightmare instead of ignoring her and forgetting she ever called? Or maybe it was the day, that instant, when his guys had gotten killed and he'd gotten his ass kicked into the sky? The day he saw that strange sun—the sun he's tried, but regrettably failed, to capture on the back of his own hand?

There must be a reason for it, some . . . *thing* to make it make sense. It must be in Mrs. S.'s deck, in the missing card she wants him to find. He glances up. On the TV he sees news of a hurricane down in the Caribbean somewhere.

"I told her," says the girl seated nearby. "I told her."

Ludwig looks over. The man holds her hands clasped in his.

"It's gonna be okay, baby." He shakes his head. "It's no big deal."

"That's what they said last time, when Georges hit. I told her we should go but she didn't wanna go and we ended up spending two nights in the fucking Superdome."

"We got a few days. We drive all night, and we'll be there by morning."

"We barely have enough for gas."

"Hey. Hey. I'll take care of you, baby."

The waitress brings Ludwig's Coke. He sits back, drinks, waits until he feels calm. He roots through his pack, fumbles through the shirts and pants and skivvies, and pulls out the envelope Mrs. S. gave him, draws from it the book, *The Origins of the Occult Tarot*. He opens it, starts to scan a page, but he gets two lines in and the spinning letters make him want to throw up.

He stuffs the book back in the envelope and the envelope back in his pack. He pays for the meal, then wanders back across the parking lot to the station. There, he gazes through the floor-to-ceiling window of the waiting area at the city and the seamless sky. His mind is bending. He feels like he's in a hall of mirrors. He blinks, shuts his eyes. When he opens them, he sees the dark blue Nissan cruising down the street. Ludwig steps away from the window, peers from behind a concrete pillar. The man is looking straight ahead. He stops at a traffic light. Ludwig steps back fast across the waiting area and out the side door. He hunches low between the parked cars, scrambles across the lot to the Mr. Dog, and sits down at a table. The waitress squints and gives him a crooked smile. She saw him leave the place only minutes before. He pulls the envelope out of his pack, reaches in to the bulge at the bottom, and fingers the thick wad of cash to reassure himself. The pregnant girl and the guy he spied earlier rise to leave.

"Hey," Ludwig says. They turn. The guy looks wary, almost threatened.

"You headed to New Orleans?" Ludwig says.

"That's right," says the guy. "What's it to you, bro?"

"Any chance I could catch a ride with you?"

"Sorry, man." The guy starts to turn away.

"Hey, hey, how 'bout if I pay my way?" Ludwig pulls two bills out of the stack. The guy and the girl stare at the hundreds. They glance at each other and back at Ludwig.

"No, man. Can't risk it. We're on a timeline."

"You just back from the Box?" Ludwig says.

Jaime frowns. "That's right. You?"

"Eight months. Thirty-seventh, right? I saw you guys in Sadr City. Saw a guy burn a whole M-Sixty into a van full of hajjis. Craziest shit. You know who that was?"

"Holy shit." Jaime grins. "Cobbs. What a crazy motherfucker. You, man?"

"RCT, man. RCT-one."

"Holy shit!" Jaime laughs and punches Ludwig's shoulder. "Holy crap!"

He hitches his head toward the exit. "C'mon bro. Where you headed?"

Ludwig keeps his head down as they walk across the parking lot. He scans the streets but he doesn't see the burned man's car. He's jittery and he wants to be on the road as fast as possible.

"What's your name?" says the guy.

"Ludwig."

"That's a funny name," says the girl. "How'd you get a name like that?"

"My dad, he was a musician, a music teacher. He loved Beethoven."

"Aha, cool." She smiles. "I'm Grace. This is Jaime."

"C'mon, brother." Jaime opens the front door of a jet-black Mustang for Grace, reaches in, and pulls up the lock to open the rear for Ludwig. Ludwig climbs in. He blinks at the shiny like-new black leather, the chrome seat belt buckles. Jaime gets in behind the wheel. Ludwig's jagging. Everything is humming. Jaime starts the car and turns to back out.

"How old's this car?" asks Ludwig.

"It's a seventy-two."

"It's beautiful."

"Thanks, man. Grace got it for me. Best gift I ever got."

Grace grins over the seat back. "It was his welcome home gift. He loves it more than his unborn child."

"Oh, baby," says Jaime as he floors the Mustang out of the parking lot. "You know that ain't so."

He keeps it at very high speed, but Ludwig doesn't mind, since that means more space behind him, more space between him and the burned man.

As they shoot west along Route 10 Ludwig watches the sun setting. He's feeling burned-out himself—incinerated, really—by terror, oxy, adrenaline. He eases into this sensation of respite and also of freedom, of the chariot ride across a landscape of wide roads and limitless sky. The smell of salt perfumes the air. Ludwig guesses it has carried from the nearby coast, the Gulf. He's dead tired, but everything is swarming in. He understands that he's in God's country, or something like it, full of bounty, a land of bloodshed and grace. He stares at his tattooed hand and remembers nights when he had prayed for solace, prayed to see any sun rising.

Marines aren't supposed to feel fear, and yet they all had. Sometimes it was all they felt. Terror had poured from them like sweat. He had smelled it in the air over the dead and under the shocking stench of spent white phosphorous that one night when he had found it hard to believe that they had taken the fight that far, that they would unleash that on *people*. Fear radiated off the Special Ops guys and the Ghebelin Guys, those pumped-up pros and killers for hire, especially in the first days of Fallujah, after four of them had been lynched, burned, and hung up on the bridge above the river. Even way back, on Parris Island, when he had been so different, just a kid really, long before he and all those other guys had known what they were getting into, only a year from having a kid of his own.

He wakes to a feeling, like falling, and finds that it's dark and cold. Grace is hunched asleep against the passenger-side door. Jaime eyes him in the rearview mirror.

"Bad dreams, bro?"

"Always." Ludwig sits up and rubs his eyes. "You need help driving?"

"Thanks. No. But my girl needs to lie down."

"Sure, man. No problem. Just pull over."

Jaime pulls over, rouses up Grace, who sighs and agrees, mumbling, that maybe she *will* be more comfortable stretched out. Ludwig waits for Jaime to help her ease back onto the seat, then he climbs into the front seat, and they're on the road again. Jaime doesn't seem to believe in a speed less than ninety. The road rushes toward the headlights. But it's okay. Traffic is light. Ludwig looks toward the horizon. The point where the headlight-lit road edges into dark is the only hint of where the land ends and the sky starts. He sees no hint of the storm he saw on the news back in Mobile.

"You okay, being back?" says Jaime.

"You mean home?"

"Hell yes."

"I can't say it's working out for me too well."

"Yeah?"

Ludwig stares at the road ahead, realizes how little he can or wants to say. "Ah, man. Where do I start?" he says. "I'm just flat-out busted down, man. My wife left me about a month ago. She took my son with her."

"Jesus. I'm sorry to hear that man."

"Thanks."

They drive on for a while.

"How old's your son?"

"What?" says Ludwig.

"Your son. How old is he?"

"Oh. Three. Three in November."

"Mmh."

"How about you?" says Ludwig. "What's it been like for you?"

"Weird, man. Real weird. The whole time I was there I *could not* get home outta my head. Know what I mean? Day and night couldn't stop thinkin' about Grace. Couldn't stop thinkin' about being with her, starting a family. Then I get back and it feels like my head's fulla bees. First months back I thought I'd lose it. Had fuckin' awful nightmares. You have nightmares?"

"Yeah."

"You wake up, like, screamin' in your head?"

"Oh yeah."

"That's what I'm talkin' about." Jaime leans over the steering wheel and stares hard like he's driving into a sandstorm although the road ahead is clear and quiet. "But things calmed down, after a while. I got a job. Grace's brother owns a place that sells batteries—all kinds a batteries. Triple-As. Batteries for cell phones, laptops, cars, everything. So I been working since March. And then, you know, we got this baby coming."

"So things got good."

"Yeah, yeah." Jaime chews his lip. He's thinking about something and Ludwig is just about to ask him what it is when Jaime comes out with it.

"Listen, man. Listen to this: This guy I knew? This guy Evershed, in my unit? Nicest guy. Real soft-spoken kinda guy. Can-do about every fuckin' thing. From Detroit. Told me once he just barely got through high school. Had this crazy kinda energy, like ADD or somethin', a fuckin' rubber ball just bouncin' all over the place. No attention span *whatsoever*. Anyway, dude signs up and he's good, a real good marine. Then one night, over there, we hit some real bad shit. Mortars come raining down on us from like three different directions: *Scchhboom. Scchhboom. Scchhboom.* And these fucking hajis come loping outta the dark like dogs, like fucking ghost dogs." Jaime shakes his head. "I was scared as shit, man. And we're in this fucking craziness for like *four* hours, *forever*. Hajjis coming again and again and again. Sun comes up and there aren't even that many bodies on the hill. I think they took a bunch of 'em away. We're supposed to move on. Guys all around geared up to ride out, and I was sitting on the ground just feeling god-awful, really sick, 'cause we lost two guys. There's this fucking

reporter there, some French guy, another guy with a camera, goin'
yada yada yada. I'm just like *Leave me the fuck alone, man. Just leave me
alone*. So Evershed walks up. I'm, like, not in the mood to talk or anything, but I can tell he needs somethin', so what the fuck, right? So
we're just sittin', dazed and jumpy, and Evershed doesn't say a word,
not a word. He just stares straight ahead. And after a while I just figure
he's fucked. Same as I am, same as we all are. So I just stare straight
ahead, too, and I wait. But after a while I can't take it anymore and
I turn and I look at Evershed and he's still staring straight ahead and
there's nothing in his eyes. Like *nothing. No thing*." Jaime falls silent
and stares ahead at the road. Ludwig waits a while.

"So what happened?" he says.

Jaime shrugs. "Nothing. Dude bucked up. Or at least I thought he
did. Got his shit together. Except something was kinda missing. It was
like all that energy, that hopped-up energy he had? It was like it got
squeezed out of him like out of a tube a toothpaste. He was in another
month, maybe month and a half before he got shot. Ramadi. Right
through the shoulder. And after that they sent him home. Drank a lot,
laughed a lot, bumped fists, then adios, Evershed outta zone."

"So he made it out okay?"

"No, man, that's just it. Come July I get this email from another
guy, buddy a mine, posted in Tampa, CENTCOM. Tells me fucking
Evershed went missing for two or three days before they found him in
a state park somewhere up in Michigan. Shot his brains out."

"Oh Jesus."

"Fucker's dead, man." Jaime brings his fist down softly on the top of
the steering wheel three times. "Dude got through Baghdad, Mosul,
the worst shit I ever seen in my motherfuckin' *life*—flown out with a
hole in his shoulder but on his feet while a whole buncha guys wound
up in body bags. Dude got out *scot-free*, man. But he didn't fuckin'

make it. Somehow, on the other side"—Jaime juts his index finger into his own forehead—"*this* fucking side—he couldn't handle it. Fucker put a bullet in his head."

"Jesus."

"Yeah, yeah. That's right. Now I got a question for you. I've got something that's been kinda bugging me since then."

"What? What is it?"

"What the fuck did he see?" Jaime turns and looks at Ludwig. He stares too long and Ludwig starts to get nervous because they're doing eighty, maybe ninety. "I mean, what the fuck did *he* see over there that I didn't see? Why is *he* dead while I'm here drivin' with my girl back there carrying my kid?" Jaime laughs. There's something cracked in it, something loose and scattershot. "I mean, why am *I* alive, while Evershed's dead in a grave somewhere up in Michigan?"

Jaime stares at Ludwig and Ludwig doesn't dare look away. He desperately wants to. Because Ludwig has been there. He's asked questions with no answers over and over again. And how often had he thought of it? The absolute darkness that lies only a hairbreadth away from all this nonsense? How doggedly had the possibility shadowed his days for months now? He doesn't want to go there. But to look away would be to abandon Jaime, ignore his fear, let go, abandon him. It's Jaime, finally, who breaks the gaze. He turns to face the road and yells before he pulls the wheel sharp. They careen away from the concrete median.

"Fuck," says Ludwig.

"Fuck. Fuck," says Jaime. "Sorry about that, man." He glances over his shoulder. "Honey? Honey, you okay?"

"Are we there yet?" murmurs Grace.

"Almost, baby." Jaime winks at Ludwig and grins like he's gotten away with something. "We're almost there."

12.

Ludwig watches Jaime and Grace, doe-eyed and pregnant Grace, peel down Route 10 at high speed. Under the screech of the tires he imagines a whispered or thought *fuck you*, and Ludwig gets it, he understands. Why would those two beautiful people speeding toward their future together want to spend more than a necessary second in the company of some fucking jamoke from Philly who can only remind them of things best forgotten?

Expelled from the Mustang's air-conditioned cocoon, Ludwig finds himself stranded in unbearable heat. He walks along the shoulder of an exit ramp and wanders down residential streets until he finds a convenience store, where he buys a fifth of whiskey and gets directions to the nearest cheap hotel, a place called L'Etteilla. He gazes up at the stained masonry and sun-blistered window shutters. He's feeling broiled and paranoid and he wants to stay indoors, so he flashes some cash and asks the man at the front desk, who looks Thai or Vietnamese, if they have anything with a fridge, or maybe a kitchen.

The guy leads him up to a suite with a kitchenette and a living room overlooking Esplanade Avenue.

As soon as Ludwig's alone, he flips on the TV and searches for any channel with news, and when he finds it, he watches and waits. But there's nothing. There's nothing about an assault or a shooting outside of Mobile, Alabama. But then it dawns on him that it might be local news. Maybe the killing of a boy in Alabama isn't news in Louisiana. Finally he can't stand it and leaves the room.

Online, on the computer in the hotel office, he searches again for news of crimes in Mobile: Mobile. Alabama. Shootings. Assault. Missing boy. Airport—one after the other and in different combinations. But nothing comes up. He sits and thinks about writing an email to the police or the FBI but scraps the idea. They'll trace it. He paid cash but he used his driver's license to check in. They'll find the hotel, the guest list, his name. He stares at the screen, feeling a new kind of low. What can he do? What can he do next?

Back in the room he calls Charlotte. The phone rings and rings but no one picks up, not even a machine. Where is she? Where's Sam? He sheds his boots, pulls the curtains shut, and turns the AC up. He takes the envelope Mrs. S. gave him out of his bag, roots to the bottom to retrieve the box of tarot cards he bought in Mobile, lies down on the bed, and pages through the book until he comes to a chapter titled "The Father of the Occult Tarot."

A French pastor named Antoine Court de Gébelin was the first person to claim that the symbols on tarot cards came from an ancient Egyptian book called *The Book of Thoth*. This was back in the 1700s, and Gébelin believed that the tarot contained all the secrets of the ancient world. Ludwig peers at an old drawing of Gébelin, riffles through the pages, and finds pictures of some tarot cards that look like Mrs. S.'s. The Gébelin name's association with the occult is hazy for most of the nineteenth century. But Théophile Ghebelin, a French steel and military armament magnate, a direct descendant of Antoine Court de Gébelin, was known to have dabbled in the occult and even to have married a famous New Orleans fortune-teller. Ghebelin's modern-day descendants were barely aware of the pastor Antoine, but the family name proved irresistible for all sorts of people with crazed agendas and lunatic fixations. Théophile's grandson Vincent, an avid collector of occult artifacts, had had an affair with a Swiss or Austrian woman who killed herself one night in 1952, setting herself on fire on the grounds of *La Marquise*. A few years later an unidentified person sent a package to the house containing a man's left hand, presented to the descendants of Antoine Court de Gébelin as a kind of offering. Ludwig thinks of the burned man, remembers his voice, the things he'd said. Is he one of these people? he wonders. Circling around this family with some deranged purpose or fixation?

He studies the photocopies that show the box with the two drawers. Wonders if the red color she described would have faded. He tears the cellophane wrap off the tarot deck box, pries it open, and spills the cards out on the bed. Their edges are clean and sharp. He pages through the small pamphlet that accompanies the cards, sees that the contents are similar to the book but in summary. He riffles through the cards, looks at the strange pictures. The cards are arranged in sequence, so it isn't hard for him to separate the major arcana cards from the rest. The count begins with a zero, the Fool. Two is the High Priestess, and so on: the Emperor, Strength, the Hermit, Death, the Devil, and more. He arranges them one by one in a semicircle around him and turns back to the book. He finds the major arcana listed in a section titled "The Meanings."

Late into the night he pores over the meanings. He'd thought that the tarot cards would be similar to the zodiac. There's nothing you can do about the sign you're born under (he, himself, is a Sagittarius). But this deck of cards, with all of the major arcana and many minor arcana, gives him the satisfying illusion of chance or choice. There's something almost democratic about it. The zodiac, it strikes him, is all about fate. Under the zodiac you are who you are—unchangeable. But these cards in front of him, these are different. There's no past in them, only what you might make of the past to plot out a future. He reads about the different ways the cards can be read, the simple three-card reading Mrs. S. had started, another kind of reading called the Celtic Cross, and another one called the Tree of Life. He does a few readings, dips into the book to interpret them. Most of the meanings are vague, bordering on meaningless. The problem, as Ludwig sees it, is how often the thing you most need to know is the last thing you really want to find out. But maybe, Ludwig thinks, the tarot gives a kind of suggestive push, a way to get things started, to move toward the answer, to focus. Maybe the tarot helps to force the issue.

He glances at his rucksack on the floor beside the bed. The oxy's in there and he wants it. He stares at the cards. The whole business starts to feel flimsy, like a sham, a self-delusion, and he remembers how he felt years back when he'd looked up at Christ on the cross and understood that although he might pray and beg and plead for his father, no one would hear him. His father was dead, as dead as his buddies in the Box. He reaches for his pack.

———————

When he wakes late in the morning, he finds that he's rolled over the cards and scattered them. He's surrounded by them. He watches his own trembling and disembodied hands take the oxy vial from the bedside table and put it back in his pack. He picks up the phone and dials for information. An automated operator prompts him for a name.

"Ghebelin," he says.

"Waveland," says the voice.

"No, no. *Ghebelin*," he says. *"Ghebelin."*

But the service or computer or whatever is on the other end runs with the mistake. Ludwig hangs up, sits with his face in his hands. After a few minutes he rifles through his rucksack and retrieves the Oakleigh Garden District pamphlet that lists Hugo Ghebelin's name. He sits and thinks, riffles through the tarot book until he finds what he remembers—*La Marquise*, the house or mansion. He washes his face and goes down to the street. A few blocks down Esplanade he goes into a store and gets directions to a tourist office on Saint Ann Street, just off Jackson Square. There, he asks an older white lady behind the counter of the tourist office if she's ever heard about the place.

"Of *course. Yes. Certainly*." She searches under the counter, pulls up a pamphlet with a drawing of a mansion on the cover, and sets it on the counter. *"La Marquise* is, *truly*, a *priceless* incarnation of the *grace* and *stately reserve* of the *postbellum* era," she says. *"Very* rare. It's in the *middle* of the *Garden* District. Today it sits on *two* acres, and our records include a *series* of deeds on that land dating from *before* the *Louisiana* Purchase. So it's *quite* unique. Many visitors from *all over* the world come to see it, and of *special* note, of *course*, is the *massive* fin de siècle ceiling, made of *stained* glass, in the *grand library*. Unfortunately, though, the owner is now *quite* old and she's requested privacy, therefore, it is no longer one of our *touring* locations. But—"

"Somebody *lives* there?"

"Yes."

"Who?"

"Well, I—I wouldn't be at liberty to say. Although it's no longer one of our *touring* locations, you *can* see the house, so long as—"

"Thanks," says Ludwig. He takes the brochure and walks out to the street. On the inside cover he finds the address. Within minutes he's in a cab. The thought that the burned man might be on his way to target whoever is at that house, Hugo Ghebelin or his family, has him on edge. A little later the cabby turns onto a quiet, wide street shaded by old trees. Ludwig eyes the numbers on the high stone walls and wrought-iron fences.

"Stop," he says.

"Here?" says the cab driver.

"Yeah. Yeah. Stop. Here."

The cabby stops. Ludwig presses back in the seat and peers out the window at the locked iron gate that looks like the one on the booklet cover. The gate and the walls adjacent are about ten feet high—a little higher than the walls surrounding the house in Mobile.

"Take me around the block."

The driver takes a turn at the corner. Ludwig studies the wall, keeps an eye open for any service gates or gaps until he spots something up ahead.

"Stop," he says.

The driver stops.

Ahead, there, on the sidewalk, Ludwig eyes a tree, an old and leafy spruce. The branches arch over the street and over the wall. One big branch arches a few feet above the top of the wall.

"Yo, fella, you gettin' out or what?"

"No," says Ludwig. "Take me back where you picked me up."

"Man, you got cash or what? You fuckin' around?"

"I got cash. Okay?" He pulls a hundred out of his pocket, waves it at the eyes in the rearview mirror. "Is that good enough? Now drive."

After Ludwig gets out on Esplanade he walks a couple blocks until he finds a pay phone in the foyer of a Thai restaurant. He dials for information and asks for the number for the address of *La Marquise*. The recording tells him the number isn't listed. He hangs up, dials 9-1-1.

"Emergency service, how can I help you?"

"I wanna report a threat."

"A threat?"

"Yeah, someone's life is in danger. I think someone's liable to get hurt."

"Okay, sir, first off I need your name."

"I don't wanna give my name."

"Well, this isn't a tip line."

"I don't care what it is. Someone needs to keep an eye on a house down here in the Garden District 'cause I think an old lady who lives there could be in some trouble."

"What kind of trouble?"

"*Trouble* trouble. Like dangerous trouble. I think someone's out to hurt her."

"Who?"

"A guy. A crazy guy. Hell, I don't know his name."

"Well, sir, I'm sorry, but this isn't a tip line. You'll have to call—"

Ludwig takes the handset and raps it hard against the pay phone again and again and again. He looks up and sees that about half a dozen diners and some of the staff inside the restaurant are staring at him. He sets the handset down and walks out fast.

In his suite, he washes his face, lies down, and stares at the ceiling. After a while he can't help himself. He pulls out the oxycodone bottle but he manages to keep himself from opening it. He lies down again. When his heart stops surging in his chest, he pulls the tarot deck out of his rucksack and splays the cards out on the bed. His eye sets on the Sun. A little boy rides a horse under the sun's watchful gaze. That sun, the sun, the boy, his son, Sam.

The strangest part of it is that he had signed up for the Marines and left for the Box to shape up, prove to himself, to Charlotte, and to a few people who had had good reason to doubt that he could be responsible and dependable. But something had happened. And when he got back, he'd found that the only thing that he really wanted—to be a good husband, to be a solid and loving father—felt impossible to achieve.

The light rises behind the rust-colored curtains. He wonders what Sam might be looking at, at that very moment, wherever he is. And Charlotte. What does Charlotte see? And where is she?

He imagines a day, a bright and sunlit morning, when he might drive them somewhere, take them on a ride in a really nice car to some suburban or countryish spot, a place with open fields where Sam can run. He would lie next to Charlotte and they would watch Sam, and Charlotte would say something like *You've done good. You've made us safe*. And he would say *Of course*, and they'd laugh and kiss. He would feel that the past was past, and he could walk into the future with Charlotte and Sam, unburdened by visions from the Box. The things he'd seen and done would be a dismal, faded memory,

———————

Late afternoon finds him spread eagle, glassy-eyed from a nightmare filled with blood and dismemberment. He washes his face and descends to the street. He finds a bar nearby and orders a sandwich and a beer, then a second beer. When he's done, he walks out to the street and hails a cab and tells the driver to take him to *La Marquise*. He walks past the wrought-iron gate. He spots two cameras perched on each side of the gate, so he sticks as close to the base of the wall as he can. The house or estate across the street is also walled, but with no visible security cameras, so he feels like he has some coverage, at least for a few minutes. He paces, then stops at the gate and peers past the iron bars.

The mansion stands at the end of a long driveway. It's four stories high and shaped like a massive box capped by a dome or cupola. It looks like something from old colonial days with a columned veranda that runs along the three sides visible from where he stands. A man, a big guy with a beard, leans against the side of a black Chevrolet Suburban, smoking a cigarette in the shade of a tree. Ludwig steps slowly away from the gate. He didn't expect to see anyone. He walks up one block, down another, away from the house. All the houses are surrounded by wrought-iron gates or stone walls. The streets are silent. Finally he screws up his courage and walks back to the block fronting the house. As he approaches he hears faint voices, footfalls, a shutting door. He walks slowly past the iron gate and does his best to look like any passing pedestrian. He sees: A tall man, Hugo Ghebelin, descending the porch stairs. The bearded man he saw earlier is holding open the passenger door of the Suburban. As Ludwig passes he hears the iron gate squeal open. By the time the Suburban shoots through he's a quarter block away standing in the shadows at the base of the wall. He can't see anything through the tinted windows. For a second he considers slipping in through the open gates, but he hesitates, retreats.

Back in his hotel room he chases an oxy with a swig of bourbon, and another swig. He turns on the TV, surfs the muted channels up and down until he settles on local news. The weatherman points to a swirling mass of clouds south of Florida. Ludwig turns the volume up. A hurricane is headed from the Caribbean toward the Gulf. The footage is mesmerizing. The storm looks big enough to swallow Florida, panhandle and all. The news switches to a TV show. Ludwig turns it off and drinks in the dark until he passes out.

When he wakes up, it's night. He stares at himself in the mirror above the sink and the mirror on the bathroom door until his face fractures into a thousand versions of itself. He turns from one mirror to the other, wonders which one might have gotten it right? Which one has a job back in Philly? Which one pays the rent, buys groceries, saves up for college and retirement? Which one carries Sam on his shoulders and walks hand in hand with Charlotte? Outnumbered and disconsolate, he sits on the edge of the bed for a while, staring at nothing. Finally he picks up the phone and dials Mrs. S.'s number.

"Hello?" It's Celia.

"It's Ludwig. Ludwig Mason. I need to talk to—"

"I'll get her."

He waits.

"Hello?"

"It's me. It's—"

"Ludwig! Where are you?"

"I'm in New Orleans."

"Are you okay? Did you call the police again? How are you?" She sounds like a grandmother, like a grandmother who actually wants to know the answer to a question Ludwig feels at a loss to answer.

"I'm getting close. I'm at a hotel, a place called L'Etteilla."

"L'Etteilla?"

"That's right."

"That's really strange. That's the name of—"

"You're crazy. You're nuts."

"What? Wh—"

"The deck, these cards. It's bullshit."

Mrs. S. makes a sound, a hesitant *eh*. But she stops, exhales, as if she's searching for words. "You sound—confused."

"I'm fine," says Ludwig. "But I've seen things. I've done things. There's nothing in those fucking cards. There was nothing anywhere to stop me from doing the things I did over there. I've done—the worst things. You say it's all about choices, but what if I've already chosen? What if I've already made terrible choices? Choices that have hurt people? What if—" He kneels. It's hard to breathe. He covers his face with his hand.

"What?" she says.

"What if there's no reason—for it? What if it's just who we are. What makes you think—we have any choice?"

"Ludwig. I understand you've seen things. I've seen things too. When you've seen these things, you have to understand—you have to *force yourself to understand* that you have a choice and you have to use it. You can't be bound by what you've done. You have to move forward and make a new way."

Ludwig stares at the dark window, the sky beyond the glass. "But what if it's too late—for some people. What if—"

"You need help. I'll send help. I'll send someone to help you."

"I don't need help. I'm fine."

"You don't sound fine. And after what happened, if there's someone threatening—"

"I—I have to go."

"But—"

"I have to go."

"Be careful, Ludwig. Please be careful."

Ludwig hangs up. He sits for a while until the echo of Mrs. S.'s voice fades. He rifles through his pack, finds the box of tarot cards, and sifts through them. She'd said they had once been a game, but someone sometime past had thought they held something more. And the burned man wants them. He studies the faces of the cards: the Moon, the Hanged Man, Justice, the Devil, and more, gives up with a curse and hurls the deck across the room.

13.

He wakes up braced to fight the urge to pop an oxycodone but finds it doesn't matter. He's still high and his mind is still *racing*. He hears Jaime's cracked laughter in his head. He feels outside himself. He's afraid he'll be flung off the ground, launched into the ceiling, maybe through it and back into the sky. He tries to focus on the silence, but it doesn't work. So he decides to stick as close to the floor as possible. He lies on the carpet beside the bed. He waits. What will happen? He'll float, he imagines, like a balloon, and rise up into the clouds, and what will happen then? Up there? Will he freeze? Will he burn? Or will he rise further, into space? Will he float up to the sun, incinerate? When he musters up the courage, he stands and walks stiff kneed to the bathroom. *Can't stay inside*, he says to the mirror. *The walls'll crush you*. So he goes down to the lobby and out to the street.

The air feels hot against his skin and his mind feels wired and weird. His head throbs. Everything looks sharp and blurry at the same time. He sticks close to the walls in case his body loses grip with the earth and he needs to leap into a doorway or grab a doorknob. The branches swing and shiver in the hot wind. He can *feel* the sound they make, as if the sound is a physical force, a tangible thing that laps at his face. The sound grows louder, more insistent. It rubs up against him, tries to suffocate him. He comes to the juncture of a narrow cobbled street. Along it runs a tall fence lined by towering oaks. Shade and quiet, residential doorways beckon. He'll find peace there, if only for a minute. Ludwig leans against a wall. It's then that he understands that the sound isn't in his head but behind him, rushing up on him. He turns and sees it but it's too late. The car, the burned man's car, bears down on him and he glimpses the burned man behind the windshield, behind a kaleidoscopic panel of reflected branches and leaves. No place to go—neither left nor right. It's as if the alleyway was custom sized for a Nissan Maxima. Ludwig has just enough time to put up his hands when everything becomes a riot of joints against vehicle: his thighs, the hood, his forearms, the windshield, his shoulder, the top of the car—and his own voice, panicked, shouting *No. Stop. Oh My God. Oh Jesus—Christ. My God.*

The end, when it comes, is a tremendous relief. He feels like he's survived a terrible dream. He rolls onto his side, props himself up on his forearm, hears and sees the car squeal and fishtail out onto the street, vanish. He kneels, stands, stumbles, leans against the fence until he must sit, accepts that he must shut his eyes, if he can just—sit. If he can just find a place to—

———————

Later, near dusk, they go toward what's left of the minaret. Powder, like fog, wafts and ebbs in the shadows and the evening light. They stagger over the concrete, the twisted rebar, the bent pipes and tangled wiring. The whole inside of the tower has collapsed. Unarmed men run about, oblivious to the shouts to put their hands up, get down, hit the ground. A stampede is under way. Tarot cards flutter like confetti. They scramble madly, wild-eyed. They could not care less about the marines, the threats, the raised guns. Bodies, half-submerged, lie in rubble and shards of glass, all powdered over with a fine coat of concrete dust. The men fall to their knees, dig with their hands.

Ludwig is astounded to see bodies everywhere, the rain of tarot cards turning and spinning in the air.

"What is it? What is this?" he asks.

Vance, who stands in the place that Chessauri has stood in other memories, in other haunted moments, stares at the tumbling cards. "It isn't about fate," Vance says, turning toward him. "It's about choices, Lud. It's about the choices you make."

14.

Ludwig wakes up. He sees a line of fluorescent bulbs. He looks to the side. He's on a bed. He's in some kind of hospital room. Or maybe he's in a hallway? He rubs his face. He's in a hallway. A poster on the wall opposite lists the top ten reasons to say no to drugs. He turns. Down the hall he sees a waiting room or sitting area. He hears the sound of a TV game show, the laughter and applause of a studio audience. He sits up. He's in a hospital gown, naked underneath. A wristband is on his arm and his name and social security number are printed on it. He winces, feels the jagged crack that runs through the center of his head. A woman, a nurse, bursts out of the doorway opposite.

"You're awake," she says.

"What happened?"

"We was just movin' you."

"How long've—I been out?"

"You don't know?"

"I wouldn't—wouldn't ask if—" He takes a deep breath. His head is spinning. The woman looks at a chart, some papers in her hands.

"I think you came in yesterday. Says you came in completely out."

"What day was yesterday?"

She looks at him. "God Almighty."

"Jesus, lady, gimme a—" He stands up but it turns out to be a bad idea. His legs buckle at the thighs. He manages to lean back against the bed. "I wasn't— Listen, you—you gotta phone here? I need a phone. I need to make a—"

"You just sit."

He gestures toward the open door behind her. "Is my stuff in there? My clothes?" He decides to chance it, lurches forward. "My pants?" His thigh burns. He winces, realizes that his hip feels off. It feels as if the sockets in his hips are out of joint.

She stands to block him but steps aside with a look of dismay as he approaches. In the room, a room that smells familiar, he finds his clothes, his shirt, his wallet, and the cell phone in a blue plastic bag on a table underneath the window. He wonders where his boots are as he dials Mrs. S.'s number.

"Hello?"

"It's Ludwig."

"Ah! Ludwig! Where are you?"

"I got hit. Someone tried to—"

"*Hit? What?* What happened?"

"I got run over."

"What? What—"

"I'm—I'm in the hospital."

"The hospital? Ludwig. Oh my God. Where? Where are you? Are you in New Orleans? I sent help but I'm not sure if they've gotten there yet. They left—"

"It's all right. I'm sorry I called. I should—lie down."

"You need help."

"No. No. It— Not if— I can get back to the hotel."

"Will you be able to get back? Do you have the money I gave you?"

"I just—need to go back there. That house. I need to check—" He feels like he's falling.

"I've sent help. Help is coming. I'll—"

"I don't—need help." But even as he says it, even as he hangs up, he knows he's lying. He needs help bad. Every time he blinks or closes his eyes, the black sun ebbs and a deep blue glow limns the horizon. *Which way to go?*, he thinks. *Which direction? Head toward the sun? Risk burning up? Or go back?* But back there is the Box and the girl in the car in the river and the bodies in the rubble. He looks at the cell phone, roots through his wallet, finds the number for Charlotte, dials.

"Hello?"

"Charlotte?"

"Ludwig."

"I—I just wanted to— I—"

"What is it? Where are you? What's wrong?"

"I'm in—the hospital. A hospital in New Orleans." Ludwig stares at the sky beyond the window. He doesn't know what more to say. He'd meant to say something, only seconds before, but he can't remember what it was and his heart isn't in it anymore. "Is Sam there?" he says.

"He's with my mom. Ludwig, you sound really weird. The caller ID says hospital. Where are you?"

"No. No," he says. "I'm—so sorry, baby." He hangs up. He takes a deep breath and the bottom of his chest heaves out and tumbles away like a patch of loose plaster. He feels that he needs something to grab hold of. He feels like he's going to shoot up into the—

"Mason. Lud. Buddy. Wake up."

Ludwig wakes up. His head's filled with concrete. He sits up. Vance crouches a few feet away from him. He stares at his friend. He would like more than anything to hug him close and to tell him how much he misses him. But he also understands that that's not how this works. This is not for real.

"Dude, you look all buggy, yo," says Vance. "You look like shit." He presses a pill into Ludwig's palm. "Here you go. This'll set you right up, buddy."

Ludwig takes the pill. What is it? Does it matter? Hugh has never steered him wrong. He swallows it, blinks. He thinks for a second about Charlotte and the baby, but he pushes it back down into the box in his mind as fast as he can. He looks up. Hugh never looks afraid, but right now he looks anxious and strung out.

"What is it?" says Ludwig.

"Check it out, man. Look over there."

They had hunkered down on the roof of an apartment building on the west side of the city. Ferrer had relieved him at dusk. Ludwig had sat down to chow and he must've fallen asleep after that.

"What's going on?" he says.

But Hugh has shuffled off into the darkness. Ludwig looks toward the wall. He sees Ferrer, Bailey, Duarden. They are sitting at the base of the wall with their legs splayed out, asleep, half-asleep, wasted and exhausted. Dario kneels at the big gun at the corner of the roof. Ludwig scrabbles toward Ferrer and Bailey. The wall overlooks the street. Beyond that stretches the west side of the downtown core. He hears Hugh's voice. "Check it out, guys."

Ludwig squints at the low horizon. What is Hugh talking about? When he reaches the wall, he sees that Ferrer is awake. He's sitting cross-legged, playing solitaire on the concrete.

"What's goin' on?" he asks.

"Chatter on the radio says they're gonna pour Whiskey Pete all up and down on this shit any minute now."

"Holy fuck."

Ferrer nods. "I know. I know." He picks up the binoculars lying on the ground beside him, hands them to Ludwig. "Glass it, man. Check it out."

The night sky above Fallujah pulses. A low drone off to his left tells him that there are helicopters, likely Cobras, beyond the river to the west, but he can't tell for sure. He hears a deep hum from the horizon, AC-130s above the desert. Is that why they'd been asked to stay put and hold this position all day? For a bombing run? They'd let only Bradleys into the city center. A lot of guys are crouched along the wall, just like him, looking out into the night, even some Ghebelin guys with their cargo pants and thigh holsters and sport wrap sunglasses set ever so fashionably on the tops of their heads. Ludwig kneels and peers over the roof wall with the binoculars.

When it starts, the phosphorous bombardment, tracer rounds dive from the indistinct shadows of planes above the city. White light bursts and arcs into the sky from the buildings and streets struck by fire—a spectacle like fireworks exploding on city blocks, splashing off buildings and rooftops. He counts the glowing plumes, counts one—two—under his breath before the thunder hits his ears.

"What you see?" says Ferrer.

"Light. Tracers. C'mon up and look, man."

"No need. Don't wanna. Who needs to see that?" Ferrer crosses himself. "Dios nos perdone."

When Ludwig glances down, he notices that the cards that Ferrer is playing solitaire with aren't playing cards, as he had thought, but cards of tarot arrayed in a cross, all turned faceup but for one, which Ferrer starts to turn with a flick of his thumb and forefinger—

The sky turns as bright as day, but only for an instant. Ludwig looks up. The air ripples and bends around him. The bombers are coming on heavy. Blocks of the city core light up with bursts of fire like exploding stars. It's hard for him to imagine what it's like where the bombs are hitting, out there, where the flares arc in bright white parabolas and where the explosions echo down the burning streets, out there in the mayhem, under the radiant night.

15.

He opens his eyes. His tongue feels pasted to the roof of his mouth. His head is throbbing. The room is dark. Is it night or is it morning?

"Ludwig?"

He turns. Sonia is sitting on the bench beneath the window. She looks worried.

He blinks. A part of him is wary. He wishes he'd woken to find Charlotte there instead. But he's thankful that he's not alone. "Hey," he says.

"Hi."

"What're you doing here?"

"My great-aunt called. She told me to come help you out."

"Told you?"

She shrugs. "It's hard to say no to her."

He tries to raise himself a little, winces at the pain. "You're tellin' me?"

"Ah." She smiles. "How're you feeling?"

"I think I'm all right."

"You don't look all right."

"I'm better than when we first met." He blinks up at the ceiling. "Every time I see you I'm laid up in a hospital somewhere."

"Every time I see *most* people they're laid up in a hospital somewhere. You need anything?"

"Water."

She rises. She has on jeans and a patterned blouse. Her hair, arranged in a big bun, floats above her head. She goes into the bathroom and comes back with a paper cup. He swallows the water. "Thanks." His head feels hollow, as if someone scraped his brains out while he was sleeping.

"I'll let you sleep."

"Please don't go."

"All right." She sits on the bench.

"Your great-aunt's a real piece a work."

"I should've warned you."

"You know what she asked me to do?"

"Yeah."

"It's crazy."

"It's money."

He swallows, thinks of the zeroes. "That it is."

She sits. After a while her silence unnerves him. He remembers the night, the symbol, the powder that wouldn't wash off.

"That night, in Germany—" he starts.

"We don't need to talk about that." Her voice sounds far away.

"Need to?" He circles in on it, decides he wouldn't necessarily be here if he hadn't been there, if that night had never happened. "When I woke up, I found all that—that stuff on me."

"I shouldn't have done that. It wasn't fair."

"But you *did* do it, right? I wasn't dreaming? I mean, what was that?"

She sits quiet. He can barely see her face in the shadows. The questions blurted out. He didn't intend to bombard her.

"You were drunk," he says. "We both were."

"That's no excuse."

"Then why'd you do it?"

"I meant it as a— It was just like, a blessing."

"A blessing?"

She turns to look toward the window. Lines of street light from the blinds cross her face. "Do you remember, Ludwig, from that night, those pictures I have, of those kids?"

"Yeah."

"I was in Baghdad for a year and a half. Most of it was in the Green Zone. I saw the worst. I know everyone there sees this stuff—you've seen it. You were *in* it. But I guess what each of us sees becomes our own private hell. I'm never gonna be able to not see what I saw. How can a kid getting hurt—? How can kids getting hurt like that—?" She covers her face with a shaking hand. "I'm not supposed to think about it that way. As a nurse, I'm supposed to do my job, not—not dwell on it. But it got to me. It still gets to me every single day. I don't know if I'm ever gonna be able to stop thinking about those kids. It got so bad." She wipes tears from her eyes.

"You know, my mom, she was born in Morocco, but her family was from all over. And my dad's family were from all over the place too. His dad was from Ethiopia and he married a Canadian woman. I grew up with all these different—things going on. Different religions. Different beliefs. All this stuff my great-aunt taught me that she'd brought with her from France. My dad's religion. Don't get me started about all the stuff my mom was into."

Ludwig blinks. "Well, if you believe in it, I guess——"

She hesitates, frowns. "Well, that's just it. At a certain point, when I was over there, in Baghdad, I stopped believing in anything. I got so—— so spun out that I got lost, inside my head, inside the darkness. I remember thinking my aunt would've been so disappointed. I'd set aside or forgotten these traditions and beliefs she'd brought with her through terrible, awful, experiences. I'd set aside everything I knew from my family. But it wasn't a choice. I just couldn't make sense of what I was seeing. I was drinking, and I needed to find a way out. I knew I had to fight to keep my mind. So I made it all my own. I invoked spirits to protect me. I'd see people coming in and out. Sometimes I'd hear that they got out all right, that everything was okay with them. Sometimes I'd hear they didn't make it. And sometimes I wouldn't hear a thing. Those were the worst in a weird way. Because I'd be so anxious, anxious and afraid for them. Worried. And I remembered everyone, each person's face, their names, and I'd just wish—I wanted to protect them, you know? I wanted to use what I knew to protect the people I loved. So I started to invoke the spirits. I summoned them to protect my friends. It was a way of giving myself power over what I was afraid of. I felt like I had the power to protect the people I knew."

She looks at him. Her face, half lit, is still and full of sadness. "I wanted to protect you," she says. "To try to protect you."

He thinks about that and glances at the back of his hand. The tattoo had mostly been inspired by the black sun he'd seen that day in Fallujah. But the compulsion to get the image graven in his skin had also been inspired by the thing she'd scrawled on him that night in Landstuhl. Now, knowing her intention, he realizes Sonia's own compulsive act may have worked exactly as she had hoped.

Overwhelmed by the realization that neither a pistol whipping nor getting hit by a car has finished the job that an IED started in Fallujah, he sinks back into the pillow. "I know you meant well. I do. The truth is, I should be dead. I should've died before we ever even met."

She steps toward him, her eyes narrowed with concern.

He hears her and he knows she means well, but her words are not a consolation, not enough. He has no energy. He has so little left to give. The struggle to prove that he can be the man he wants to be has proven futile. He thinks of the burned man and whoever lives in the house in the Garden District. He's probably too late to do anything to help. He puts his hands to his face and it breaks out all at once, past the dam that's held back shock, shame, anguish, and dismay. All of it comes out. Sonia steps to him and touches his face. She takes his hand in hers and holds it tight.

"Don't go," he says.

"I won't, " she says. "I won't leave you."

He sits up and blinks at the sun. At the bottom of the hill, three tour buses line the highway's edge. The surface of a lake shimmers in the distance: Mileh Tharthar. It looks so vast, it could just as well be the sea.

They are north of Ramadi, south of Sāmarrā, halfway between the Tigris and Euphrates Rivers. Long lines of women and children, some old people, wait to board the buses. Families and loved ones of a few key Ba'athists, getting shipped off in something akin to a mass relocation or witness protection program. Their lives will never be the same. Ludwig blinks and stares. Where are people like that supposed to go? he wonders. Everything about them, their clothes, their language, the very food they eat, is from here. He understands that their blood runs from the Tigris and Euphrates. Where else is there for them?

He rubs his eyes and scans the sky, the desert, the lines of tanks and Humvees and two Chinooks parked off beyond the buses—everything is coated with a fine rust-colored haze or dust that makes him fear that he's burned his retinas, that the damage will be permanent. For the rest of his life he'll see the world coated with a fine coat of red dust.

"Movin' out soon," says Ferrer.

Ludwig turns. The sun is a red hazy ball above the horizon. Ferrer has set up a crude but proven-effective hydration system consisting of five white tube socks, filled with water bottles, over which he pours water to cool them down. Ludwig checks his gear, puts on his pack, looks up. Wonder is holding court a few feet away, talking about the deficit, always on about the deficit, and how rising, unfettered, unchecked national debt will ruin the country, destroy it once and for all and finish the job al-Qaeda started. Ludwig looks away. It is easy to get spun into Wonder's wonderful conceits. They are always provocative, always outlandish and compelling, often enraging to the more conservative members of the crew who would seem to prefer not to dig too deep into the reasons they are in the Box. Ludwig, like many of the others, looks on Wonder with a mix of awe and adoration. But right then Ludwig is feeling delirious, and he's trying to keep it together. He is sorting through the box inside his head, the box in which he keeps the visions and sensations of his life outside the Box: pictures of Charlotte, her face, the sound of his new baby boy Sam's moist breathing and Charlotte's laughter. Where is the image of the boy's face? What does he look like? Where the hell did he put the picture of his boy?

"Whattya talkin' about?" says Ferrer.

Ludwig blinks. He doesn't recall saying anything out loud. "Just—tryin' to remember what he looks like," he says.

Ferrer cocks an eyebrow. "You hydratin', man?" He looks around in disgust. "See? See that? That's what I'm talkin' about! Lud's brains is fried." He shakes his head and pours more water on the socks. "You fuckers mock, but that's why I tell all y'all all the damn time to keep hydratin'.*"*

Ludwig blinks. His lips do feel dry, but then so does his soul. He feels like his soul has withered and dried up and blown away with the desert sand. Then he sees it: far beyond the buses and the Chinooks, but closer than the low ridge of the horizon, a wall of sand, a roiling mass of sand like the surface of a sea or lake set vertical, moving toward them.

"Jesus," he says.

But Ferrer doesn't turn. He's sorting through his pack. He doesn't see what's bearing down on them. He doesn't see the trouble on the way.

"You sound sick, man," Ferrer says absently. "Maybe you just rest a while longer. You sound like—"

"But look," says Ludwig. "Check—" He swallows. It's painful to swallow. The fine red dust has gotten into his throat. He tries again, but he's afraid he might choke on it. He has to warn someone, "Check it out," he whispers.

Ferrer looks up, glances at Ludwig, follows Ludwig's gaze to the storm on the horizon.

"Oh my God," he says.

16

Light streams into Ludwig's eyes. He opens them. He blinks. A man seated in a chair a few feet away from where he last saw Sonia is staring at him. The man's blond hair crests down into a neat widow's peak. He's wearing a white shirt and a necklace with a small, round, turquoise pendant. He looks very much at ease and he also looks familiar. Ludwig strains to remember where he knows him from. *Whatshisname? Whatshisname?* Then he gets it, drags it up from the silty current of his brain. *That's right. That's right.* It's the guy he met in Landstuhl, the guy who gave him a ride back to the hospital from Sonia's place: it's Otto.

"Hey," says Ludwig.

"Allo," says Otto.

Ludwig sits up. His mouth tastes sour. "Otto? Right?"

Otto nods. "That's right, Good to see you're alive. There is food there, water too, if you want some."

Ludwig looks at the tray beside the bed: a bottle of water, a foil-covered plastic cup of orange juice, a small container of yogurt, and a plastic cover that he lifts to reveal a breakfast of toast and fluffy scrambled eggs. He leans back against the pillows, takes a deep breath, and wipes the sweat on his face. *Oh God*, he thinks.

"Are you okay?" says Otto.

Ludwig lurches to the bathroom. His right side feels bruised, brutalized. It feels as if he's been pummeled with a baseball bat. He kneels in front of the toilet but nothing comes out. He can't breathe. *Oh goodness*, he whispers. He lies down on the tile floor and passes out. Then he showers. When he walks out of the bathroom, Otto gestures to Ludwig's clothes, folded neatly on the counter by the sink in the corner. Ludwig finds his wallet, belt, and keys in a small plastic bag beneath his clothes. He starts to dress.

"There is a message for you."

"Where?"

Otto points to the counter. "There."

It takes something out of Ludwig to cross the room, but when he reaches it, he unfolds the sheet of paper. Someone has written *Charlotte called. Call her.* And underneath it is the number Charlotte gave him when she left with Sam.

"Did you take this?" Ludwig says.

"No. Sonia must have. Maybe last night or earlier this morning."

Ludwig stares at the message. When did Sonia leave? He must have fallen asleep. And how did Charlotte find out he was there, in New Orleans? Did he call her? *I must have*, he thinks. *I must have*. He strains to remember what she said, what he might have said, but his memory stops at a point like a busted clock. He gives up when the effort threatens to widen the crack inside his head.

"I gotta get outta here," he says.

"Are you sure you can?"

Mrs. S.'s voice calls his name through a haze as he finishes dressing. He thinks of Charlotte and Sam. How will he get to them? How will he get them back? He remembers the guy Jaime told him about who blew his brains out up in Michigan. Had that guy wondered where he was? Had he given up trying to figure it out? Decided he would never know?

"I don't know how much you remember," says Otto. "About the night we first met."

"I remember." Ludwig looks up. The room tilts and rights itself. Otto is sitting with his legs stretched out in front of him, very still, very watchful. "What of it?"

"I think I warned you—"

"This has got nothing to do with Sonia."

"Ah."

"I'm just tryin' to get home."

"You have a long, long way to go, my friend."

"Well, thanks."

"I don't mean to be—pessimistic. I say it only because I feel I have been somewhere like where you are now."

"I doubt that."

Otto shrugs, smiles. Ludwig spots a pair of new black boots on the floor beside the bed.

"Whose are those?"

"Yours. We bought them for you. I mean, Sonia did."

Ludwig strains to remember where his own shoes could be, gives up. "You came here—from Germany?"

"No, no, man. I was in Dublin."

"What were you doing there?"

"Ah." He tilts his head back and yawns. "A girl. It didn't work out."

"Was she with you?"

"The girl?"

"No. No. Sonia."

"No. She was in Atlanta. She called and asked for help." He rises, studies a laminated sheet posted on the wall under the television. "We knew the hotel, from her aunt, but we had to check the hospitals. We're here to help you. Whatever you need, man. I thought perhaps—"

"Where is she?"

"Sonia?"

"Yeah."

"She went to rent a car." Otto pulls on the blinds with a finger and peers out the window. "I hope the two of you have gotten over that shit that happened between you in Landstuhl."

"It's nothing."

"But it's strange, no?"

"It's nothing. I said already—" He takes a deep breath. "Listen. She called me. She got me this job with Missus S. That's why—that's why I'm here."

Otto nods, looks around the room. "Ah, yes, I see that everything has worked out for you, then."

"Huh." Ludwig swallows. He knows that Otto has a point but the jab annoys him. "I know why I'm here. Do you know why you're here? 'Cause it sure as hell isn't for my sake."

"I told you, Sonia asked me to come."

"So you come, like that? At the drop of a hat? You still love her, don't you?"

Otto's eyes narrow. "That is—very complicated."

"I'm sure it is." Ludwig feels another surge of nausea. He wipes the cold sweat from his brow. "What day is it?"

"Saturday."

"Jesus."

"The nurse said they thought you'd been mugged or something."

Ludwig clenches his eyes shut: The dog. The boy running in the tall grass. The burned man. The car gunning toward him. The mansion. *Some old lady*, he thinks. He rises, winces, limps to the window, and pries open the blind slats. Below is a scene of mayhem. He spots three cop cars at the end of the block, ambulances lined up around the corner leading to the hospital's main entrance, a man and a woman boarding up the windows of a coffee shop across the way. "What the fuck is going on?"

"Oh, shit," says Otto. "Of course. Of course. I'll show you." He stands and reaches up to turn on the television hanging from the ceiling. "You have to see this. Watch this. It's crazy. People are abandoning the city like it is collapsing, leaving everyone behind. I've never seen anything like it before." He points to the TV. "Look."

The news is on low volume and it looks bad. The screen is a strobe of fast cutaways and scrolling video ticker tape. A threat of impending crisis projects into the room. The palms along the coast bend and whip in the wind behind the weather lady.

"Holy shit."

"You see? It is quite unbelievable. We have to go. There may not be flights, but if Sonia gets a car, we can drive out."

"What're you talking about?"

Otto frowns. "I'm talking about driving, man. Going. Getting the fuck out of here."

"No. No way, man. I'm still working this thing."

"Are you crazy? A massive storm is coming. The city is evacuating."

"Listen, man—there's a guy, this crazy, fucked-up guy. He nearly killed me. He's—"

"I know."

"What? How—"

"Sonia told me. She said someone attacked you or something. What happened?"

"This guy just drove up. I was walking down the street in Mobile, and he drove up, and he had a gun and he told me to get in the car."

"Who was he?"

"I don't know."

"But didn't he say anything?"

"Yeah, but—" Ludwig feels like he'll be sick again. "He just drove to this stretch by the Gulf outside Mobile and we went into this place with warehouses. He told me to back off, to quit doing this job for Missus S."

"*Mein gott.* What did you do?"

"I—I ran."

"But did you call the police?"

"Yeah. I did. But— Just listen. This guy—the guy who did this—I have to stop him. I think I know where he's headed—this house, in the Garden District here, it's called the Marquise, at First and Chestnut. But some old lady lives there. He's crazy. He could go after her. I have to—"

"Ah. *Mein gott.*"

"I've gotta stop him."

"You have got to call the police is what you've got to do. Tell *them* what you know."

"I did. I did. But I can't get too close to it. How'm I supposed to explain what I'm doing down here? *I* don't even know what I'm doing here." The pain slices through his side, like a knife cutting at his guts from the inside.

"You should sit," says Otto. "Do you want anything? Something else to eat?"

Ludwig sits. What he wants more than anything is to sleep. But he has to go. The burned man is out there. "I'm starving. A sandwich, some juice. Anything."

"Yes. There's a cafeteria downstairs. I'll get you something." Otto rises, goes to the door. "Rest if you need. I'll be back in a few minutes. Then we'll get the fuck out of here, eh?" He closes the door behind him.

Ludwig waits for a count of ten and goes to the door. He peers out, looks left, right, sees no sign of Otto. A few steps down the hallway the nurse he saw when he first woke eyes him from behind the nurses' station.

"Where're you goin'?"

"Out."

"You can't— Stop."

Ludwig braces himself against the wall. "Just going to get some fresh air." He lurches and swivels his aching hip forward.

"Call security." Her tone is urgent. A metallic clatter signals that she's risen from her chair. "Beth." She's yelling. "Beth. Call security."

He jabs the elevator down button, cursing frenziedly the whole while. The elevator door opens and he lunges in. He scrabbles at the button for the first floor. His curses turn to panicked pleas and exhortations when he spots the nurse headed toward him. But the door closes just in time. After finding the lobby, he pushes through a revolving door and stops fast. The sky is stone gray and the air feels damp and electric against his skin. He glances back. A security guard is walking fast across the lobby toward him. Ludwig lunges across the sidewalk and into a cab standing at the curb. The cabbie sets down his paper.

"Esplanade, buddy," says Ludwig. "Esplanade and Rampart, fast."

The cabbie takes off. A few minutes later they're stopped in a gridlock of cars and minivans.

"Crazy, huh?" says the driver.

"Yeah," says Ludwig. He turns away from the cabbie's gaze in the mirror. He's not interested in making conversation. But it *is* crazy. So far as Ludwig knows, hurricanes hit the Gulf every year. The sky is bleak and forbidding and the wind whips and buffets the cab—but what's with all the panic?

Ludwig asks the cabbie to stop and he goes into a convenience store. He gulps a bottle of water straight off the shelf. After he pays for it he gets in the cab. He'd meant to go to the hotel, get his things, but the bottle of pills is in his bag and he knows that's all he wants and he knows he doesn't want it.

"Changed my mind about Rampart," he says.

"All right, but you hear this on the radio? I gotta get outta this. Wife wants me home. Where you wanna go?" says the driver.

"Take me to the Garden District."

17.

When Ludwig did surveillance on the house, the gates were shut and forbidding and he'd thought if he had to enter, he would have to go over the wall. But now, in a midday as dark as night, the gates stand wide open.

He watches the cab drive off. The street is quiet. No cops, no civilians. Everything looks clear. He hobbles across a stretch of yard and crouches against a tree trunk, watching the house.

The windows are all dark but the veranda is lit and the cupola glows with a muted amber light. The Suburban stands in the driveway. He watches and waits but sees no movement in the windows or outside except for the brutal wind and a dismal, rising rain.

He closes his eyes. *Why am I here?* he thinks. He was supposed to find the deck, bring it back to Mrs. S., get the money she offered him. But he's here, now, in the storm, thinking he can help protect whoever's in the house from a man he's not even sure exists outside of the haze of an oxy-fueled bender. He opens his eyes. "Okay," he whispers.

Hobbling around the side, Ludwig nearly collides with a woman in pajamas. She screams and holds up her hands. She's older, maybe fifty, and she's terrified, plain to see. She has on pajamas and white sneakers.

"Who are you?" he says.

"Carlotta. Carlotta. Did Mister Petra call for you? The phone is out. I don't know if it's 'cause of the storm. Thank God Mister Petra reached you. I don't know what's happening in there. I don't have— I can't believe this is happening." Her face collapses. She looks like she's going to cry. Ludwig realizes she's not wearing pajamas. They're hospital scrubs.

"It's okay. It's okay. Calm down." He touches her arm. She's shaking. "Where'd you come from?" he says.

"Inside. Just inside. I just—I just ran out. Oh my God."

"Who's in there?"

"A man— A man, and a— Oh my God, who is he? I saw him just for a second, walking across the hall. I can't believe this is happening. My son. I have a son. I need my son—"

"Your son's in there?"

"No. No. My son's at home." She's shaking. "He went upstairs. I was—"

"Who went upstairs?"

"Mister Petra. I was in the kitchen and I heard Mister Ghebelin shouting." She freezes, looks back and forth. "Oh, his voice. Where's Mister Petra? We were just eating dinner in the kitchen and then he went to help him and then I heard them yelling and then someone was screaming. Oh God. Oh God. I hid. I hid in the kitchen. In the pantry. But I saw him, the man, in the hall." Carlotta starts to cry.

"Who's Mister Petra?"

"He's Mister Ghebelin's friend. His—his bodyguard. He's the security man from the company."

"Who's in there right now?"

"Mister Petra, if he's not with you, and Mister Ghebelin and Missus G. and that—that *man*."

"Who's Missus G.?"

"Missus Ghebelin. This is Missus Ghebelin's house."

"Ah," says Ludwig. "Listen, I'm going in there. You understand? I'm going in. There's a crazy motherfu—excuse me—a crazy guy somewhere up there and I gotta stop him."

She puts her hands on his shoulders. "Don't. Don't," she moans.

"You saw him? A tall guy, right?" he says. "With a burn all up the side of his face?"

Her eyes go wide. "You saw him too?"

"Yeah." He guides her toward the wall near the gate. It offers no real shelter, but it's away from the house. "Listen. You stay here. If you see him, if anything starts, any craziness, just run, okay? You understand?"

Carlotta nods.

Ludwig goes around the corner of the house and crouches toward the front door from the side. It stands half open. He touches it, peers in, sees no movement, hears no sound.

He enters a hall with white marble floors. The walls surrounding are sky blue and lined with brass sconces. Along the walls hang what Ludwig suspects are paintings, but they're all draped over with sheets that look as if they've hung there for a hundred years. He pads across the hall to the foot of a wide wood stairway.

Across from the stairs Ludwig sees a dark room. He goes to it, enters. Light flashes and he sees furniture, a tall mirror above a giant fireplace. He limps to the fireplace, studies the tool stand, and pulls out a heavy brass poker. He goes into the hall and climbs to a landing. Double doors stand open across the hall. He walks in and sees a man seated far across the room beside a table set on a platform or dais.

Music plays. Ludwig hesitates, moves forward with the poker brandished over his shoulder. The music is Beethoven's 131, a piece his father would often play at night sequestered in the basement when he thought everyone was asleep and he could drink in solitude. Ludwig feels like the night is moving around him, or as if he's being pulled into each strange and surreal moment. He breathes deep. He's felt this way before: back in the Box. When he first met Mrs. S. The last time he walked into the room in which this very music had played on his father's stereo.

He pads across Persian rugs; past tables piled high with books, strange painted icons, and old photographs, brass instruments, small marble statues, remnants of animals—bleached bones, a stuffed monkey with manic, dusty glass eyes. The room smells of tobacco smoke and perfume. Ludwig skirts a crimson settee, descends two broad steps into an octagonal well that's filled with richly colored cushions surrounding a low round table. A stained glass dome vaults above, made up of narrow wedges that radiate from the center, held together by a thin black tracery in a web of stunning size and elegant symmetry, all vibrancy and color. Each wedge depicts a symbol: the Lovers, the Hanged Man, Death, the Emperor, and more. Ludwig spots them all. Only a week before, he wouldn't have known the symbols for what they were. There must be lights along the circumference shining on it, or maybe bulbs above the stained glass. How else can it glow so brightly? He hesitates, stops. Could Mrs. S.'s missing symbol be up there? He scans the wedges, but he doesn't see anything he doesn't recognize. All twenty-two are there. Oddly, or maybe not so odd at all, one extra wedge is blank, filled in with amber-colored glass.

The man on the dais is slumped over. A pistol, a Glock, lies on the carpet a few feet away. On a table close by, a tarnished brass speaker sprouts from an old Victrola like a petrified mutant flower. Ludwig lifts the needle, and Beethoven's sorrowful string quartet comes to a scratching halt.

The man's wrists are tied behind the chair on which he sits. His bare chest and his white shirt, unbuttoned to the navel, are stained with blood. His mouth hangs slack. His eyes are open but there's nothing left in them. Ludwig sees that it's the driver. He steps forward, peers at the mournful face, passes his hand gently over the man's brow and feels the feathery bristles of his lashes against his palm as his eyes shut closed. Then he drops the brass poker and takes the gun.

18.

Each step feels like a tug on a hook in Ludwig's heart as he climbs up the narrow flight of stairs. The burned man is up there. He knows it.

He comes to a hall lit by a derelict chandelier. Down one end, past closed doors, stand abandoned work lights, and ladders, and tarps covering boxes, or maybe furniture. A strip of the ceiling has fallen away, revealing blackened beams from which water runs with the strength of a half-turned faucet into a hole in the floor below. Down the other way Ludwig sees two closed doors, walls covered with old wallpaper, a pattern of white and yellow and rose-colored carnations. Wind pounds plywood boards that have been put up against high windowpanes at the far end. Ludwig eyes the doors and sees a line of light beneath one. He sidles against the wall until he reaches it. He hears muttering, a man's voice. It's the burned man:

"There's gotta be a reason. The killing. All the killing—it just goes on and on and on and my hands are dripping with it. Don't you see?

I've killed women and children. But I can clean myself, can't I? I can *avenge* them by destroying you."

Silence falls, followed by footsteps, the rasp and rattle of someone struggling to breathe. Ludwig leans forward. The door is closed. He kneels and clenches his jaw at the pain in his hip. He swallows, lets the pain pass until he can stand again. He turns the knob, pushes the door, and peers in.

The room is filled with firelight from another massive fireplace. Close by, on a high-backed chair, sits a man facing a giant, canopied bed. On the far side of the bed stands the burned man, studying the screens of a bank of medical monitors.

Silence gives way to the piercing wail of a machine alarm. The burned man holds a finger poised above a monitor screen, touches it. The alarm volume falls and he proceeds to push buttons down the row. The waves of light scan flat on the four screens and the alarms give way to the sound of the crackling blaze in the fireplace.

Ludwig, expecting a reaction, looks toward the man in the chair but the man sits motionless and Ludwig senses that there's something wrong there, something is off. He looks back toward the bed.

The burned man leans over a very old woman. The woman's eyes are open but she's not moving. Her brown face floats in a thick pool of silver hair, and her form, under the emerald sheet, is as slender as a child's. The man draws a pillow from beside her, holds the edges tight and eases it toward her face with an expression of deep regret and mourning.

Startled, Ludwig pushes the door open wider. It creaks on its hinges. The burned man looks up. Ludwig freezes. The burned man crouches behind the bed. Ludwig kicks the door wide open.

"Put your hands up," he yells.

The burned man rises and hoists a sawed-off shotgun to his shoulder. First comes the blinding light followed by the roar. Two shots blow apart the wall beside Ludwig. The gun almost falls from his grip. He rolls to the floor and shimmies fast back into the hall. His breath rushes out of him as he leans back against the wall and checks to see where he's been hit. His hip, his thigh, his shoulder are burning, but he finds no rip, no blood, no wound. He hears the man reload.

"Come on out, kid. Put down the gun. I'm not gonna hurt you."

Ludwig tightens his grip on the Glock. A long silence follows. He listens for any sound of the burned man approaching.

"Listen, kid, listen. You there?"

Ludwig glances at the water dripping from the ceiling into the floor below.

"Did I hit you?" The burned man's voice is close, low, almost friendly. "Kid. I didn't mean it personal. This is just a big misunderstanding. There's no reason to do this. I'm not gonna hurt you."

Ludwig hears the floor creak. "No! No! You ran me over. Stay back," he yells. "Stay back. And don't go near that lady. I'll kill you. I'll fucking kill you if you hurt her."

He hears a breath, like a sigh. The man sounds too close.

"What's done is done. C'mon, kid. C'mon. Listen. Will you just listen to me?"

"What happened to that kid outside of Mobile?"

"The kid that ran?"

"Yeah."

"I chased him. Thought he was you. And when I reached the edge of the field I watched him scuttle across the highway. Ludwig, I need you to listen."

"What? What is it?"

"I just wanna float something by you. I want you to imagine something, a kinda—like a scenario. Imagine this kinda scenario where a young guy, could be any guy, decides he's gonna sign up, enlist, actually go to some foreign country and kill total fucking strangers in a completely made-up war. It doesn't have to be you. It could be any fucking fool."

"Fuck you!"

His shout echoes and fades under the sound of the rain and the wind hammering against the plywood boards at the end of the hall.

"Live with it, kid. I have and I've got the scars to prove it. Live with the possibility that you went over there for *nothing*. No reason, no sense, just *nonsense*. This shit's happened before. But you wouldn't know. You're too young or too stupid to know it. Remember the *Maine*? To hell with Spain? The Tonkin incident? Iran-Contra? Shit gets made up *all the time*. But this con is up. I've stopped it. Nothing I could do about the father but I got the son."

Ludwig hears the floor creak. He opens his eyes, terrified, exhausted. "Stay back." A weary, nihilistic chuckle bursts out of him. He can't catch a break, from dreams, from himself, from a crazed man with a shotgun on a rampage. He aims at the open doorway beside him.

"You see?" says the burned man. "*I* went *into* the illusion. Don't you see? And then I came back, and I realized that all this—*this* is an illusion too. *CEOs.* Contractors like our friend Hugo here. *Po-li-ti-cians.* They rig the whole thing up like a movie or a play. That's what these people do. They *create* the illusion, the illusion of what we want. They manipulate and prod and steer us toward our worst instincts. And the whole time they're reaching into our pockets. All these cons just jonesing for a piece. Rip-off artists, all of 'em. You were there. Most people don't know. But you know, kid. You *know* what I'm talking about. You've *seen* war and killing, just like I have. You've *seen* the manipulation—what they manipulate people into doing. And for what? Who wins? Who profits? *They* do. You've *seen* the other side."

Ludwig blinks and swallows. "You're crazy."

"Am I? Think about it, kid."

Ludwig's mouth is dry and his belly feels hollow. The gun trembles in his hand. "I already have. I've thought about it plenty. And whatever happened over there—all that—even if it was a lie, at the end of it I *chose* to go. No one made me. The things I saw—the things I did—they're all on me."

A silence falls, cradled by the rattling of the windowpanes, the creaking of the house. Finally, Ludwig hears a footfall.

"Huh," says the burned man. "I guess that's another difference between us then. Not everyone has a choice."

The floor creaks again. Ludwig's mind blazes with the idea that he will have to kill the man to stay alive. "Wait. Just—just wait a minute. I'm not— Stay back!" he yells.

The creaking doesn't stop. The man is headed toward the door. Ludwig scrambles to his knees. "Stop!" he yells. "Don't do this!" But the man keeps coming. Ludwig rolls into the doorway, aims, and gets two shots off. The man runs, dives behind the chair, and looms up fast. Ludwig rises to his hands and knees, but he has no time to back out into the hallway. The burned man tracks him and shoots. A dresser buckles and splinters. Bottles explode; a big oval mirror shatters. A lamp with a stained glass shade careens into the wall. Ludwig dives to the floor beside the bed. *Oh God*, he thinks. The pain in his side radiates through his body. He listens but hears nothing. He peers over the edge of the bed and sees the man streak out the door.

Ludwig follows. He darts across the hall and looks down the staircase but sees no one there. He goes back into the bedroom, walks toward the chair, peers close at Hugo Ghebelin's now-familiar face. The handle of an old bayonet knife sticks out of the center of Ghebelin's chest, embedded to the crossguard in his crisp, blue, blood-stained dress shirt. A submachine gun lies on the carpet beside the chair. Ludwig looks toward the door but sees nothing. He leans forward, peers into Ghebelin's face. Ghebelin blinks up at him and Ludwig freezes.

"*Who*—the *fuck*—was *that*?" Ghebelin whispers.

"I—I don't know."

Ghebelin blinks again. He starts to shake. Ludwig thinks that he's going to say more, but blood pours out of Ghebelin's mouth instead of words. A terrible sound follows, a rattling that overtakes Ghebelin's face and hands until he sighs and settles into silence.

Ludwig feels like he's going to be sick. His own hand shakes as he checks for a pulse and finds nothing. He crosses to the bed. The monitor screens are blank. He plugs in the machine, and the monitors light but he sees no waves, no movement. He leans over the old woman. Her eyes are closed. He lifts her hand and touches her wrist. Expecting nothing, he's startled to feel her pulse, thumping fast, like the panicked motion of a small animal, first hesitant, then circling, then burrowing away from the threat of his touch until it fades and flees forever. *She's gone*, he thinks. *She's gone*. Who is she? he wonders. Is she the daughter of the Mrs. Ghebelin he had read about? Her mahogany face is regal, serene, mesmerizing, like the sculpture of a goddess polished by time. He studies her face. He feels like something vast and great has ended but he wishes he understood what it was. Is it just the life of this woman? No small thing. But he senses that something else is gone as well. What could it be? He feels a rush of so many things, of all the things his heart mourns and has mourned each day since he got out of the Box: the loss of dignity, of grace, of integrity and faith, his own and the world's, each struck down one by one until their passing has come to feel like the sun has vanished from the sky or the earth has fallen out from under him.

As he rests her hands on the sheets, one atop the other, palms down, he wonders what unknown thing has vanished like the last of a language or a species of bird or flower or a part of the soul. And what will replace it? For the loss of something must mean the birth of something new, no?

He glances at Hugo Ghebelin dead in the chair. He'd meant to stop all of this from happening but he hasn't stopped anything at all. His eyes sweep the sundered wood and mirror shards and settle on a photograph in a silver frame. In the photograph a woman who looks exactly like the woman in the bed, but younger, stands in old bridal finery beside a man who looks like Théophile Ghebelin. Beside the photo is a brass bowl in which he finds small black beans, two copper-colored coins so worn, the faces on the obverse of each are almost smooth, four feathers, one black with white speckles, one white, one iridescent blue, and another pale green, a pan or plate of black metal the diameter of his thumb, and what he thinks at first are oddly shaped stones or pebbles, smooth as marble before he sees that they are bones. And behind the brass bowl sits a red box with two drawers and tiny gold drawer handles shaped like the faces of birds with hooked beaks. What had Mrs. S. said those birds were called? He takes the box and bolts down the stairs.

19.

Smoke billows up the stairwell. In the front hall Ludwig sees a rippling wall of flames in the room with the fireplace. The curtains are on fire. When he finds Otto standing in front of the house, he knows that the strange dream of the night hasn't ended.

"There's a lady—"

"She ran off," shouts Otto. "I tried to stop—"

"What?" Ludwig steps past Otto. He looks up the path but he can't see far. The rain stings his face, and wind unlike anything he has ever felt pushes the trees sideways. He staggers and leans into it to stay on his feet. Is the woman safe? What was her name? Carlotta, she'd said. Where could she have gone? The storm has fallen on New Orleans.

"She just took off across the street." Otto grabs his arm. "Listen, we have to go. Police are on the way." He squints over Ludwig's shoulder. "My God," he says.

Ludwig turns to look. *La Marquise* is engulfed in flames. Thick smoke rises and spirals from the windows. The blaze runs along the portico and leaps up to the ceiling as it consumes the bottom floor of the mansion. Ludwig listens to the creak and pop of glass and wood, watches the flames, and wonders if the burned man is still inside.

"He's burning it down," he says.

"Who?" asks Otto.

"The guy. The guy I told you about."

Otto tugs at his arm. "We have to go. The car, up here."

Ludwig follows Otto. He stops when a figure in a dark hoodie rushes toward them up the path. It's Sonia. She stares at him with wide, stunned eyes.

"Ludwig."

"Sonia," he says.

She touches his face. "C'mon. Fast." She turns and sprints ahead.

The pain shoots up Ludwig's hip as he runs. He glances back at the wide-open front door, the inferno inside, and hesitates. *What the——?* He thinks. *There, there——*a figure jumps through the flames. "Run!" he yells.

Ludwig hobbles after Otto and Sonia, toward the open gate. Down the asphalt path they run, out of the yard, into the street. Otto waves him toward the open front-passenger door. Sonia climbs in the driver's seat.

"Get in. Get in. Get in," she yells.

Ludwig throws the red box in and jumps into the car. He turns to call for Otto when he sees the burned man step out from the gated entrance of the Ghebelin estate with the shotgun level at his hip. The shotgun roars. Otto wheels around. Arms splayed, he slumps against Ludwig's door. Another blast follows. Otto shudders as he slides down the side of the car.

"No!" screams Sonia.

The burned man leans against the gate to reload.

"Go!" shouts Ludwig. "Go. Go. Go."

Sonia floors it. Ludwig cranes around. Through the rear window he sees Otto in the street. He punches the dashboard. "We can't leave him," he yells.

Sonia stops fast and they look back. There lies Otto, still in the road. But there's no one else, only the sound of the engine and the driving wind and rain in cones of streetlight.

"Oh God. We've gotta go back," Sonia yells. "We have to help him."

"Go back. Put it in reverse and go back."

Sonia puts the car in reverse. Ludwig opens his door as they get closer to Otto. He plans to lean out and pull Otto in. But as they draw near, the burned man steps out from behind the gate and levels the gun at the car. The rear window shatters.

"Go. Go." Ludwig shouts. "Go now."

Sonia careens toward a yellow dump truck standing in the middle of the intersection. She jerks at the wheel and swerves around it. The driver-side window shatters, but she brings the car full circle and then they're moving fast. Ludwig looks back. He squints to see the man but the road behind them is pitch-black. Ahead, the windshield wipers thrash against the rain. They ride in silence for a while. Sonia turns and turns again into dark and windswept streets, driving with a graceful efficiency. After a while Ludwig feels like he can breathe again. He settles back into his seat.

"My God. My God. We lost him," he says. "Jesus Christ. Jesus."

"I'm hit."

"What?"

Sonia sits collapsed against her door. Her hands hang limp on the wheel. "I think I'm hit." She looks breathless and sick.

Ludwig reaches across and touches her far shoulder. She winces. The fabric of her hoodie feels shredded, wet and warm. He draws his hand back and it's covered with blood. Sonia looks as if she's falling asleep, but they're still moving fast.

"Jesus. Sonia. We need to get you to a hospital."

She blinks, nods. She looks calm, at peace. "Okay," she says.

They crash. The dashboard hurtles toward Ludwig but he has enough time to understand that he has it wrong—the dynamics. He understands that *he* is hurtling toward *it* just as his head smashes against it.

———————

When he gathers himself up, he finds Sonia draped over her air bag. Her face is covered with a fine white powder and her nose is bleeding.

Ludwig checks Sonia's neck and her eyes before he gets out. How much time has passed? The hood of the car is embedded in the rear of a minivan. The minivan is embedded in a fence that has bent and twisted beneath its front bumper. He looks up. He isn't sure how far they've driven. How far away is the burned man? And then there's the storm. He can barely keep his eyes open in the driving rain. He goes around to the driver's side and opens the door. The wind is so powerful that he has to push his whole weight against the door to keep it open.

When he has Sonia's head against his shoulder, he wipes what blood he can from her slack face. "Sonia," he whispers. "Sonia."

She looks at him, probes his face with eyes half open. "Mmmmm," she says.

"Wait," he says. "Wait."

He runs to the minivan. The van stands at an angle on top of a bent section of iron fencing. The side door is wide-open. He looks inside, expects the worst, but finds instead in the soaked interior a few abandoned toys, a pale blue blanket, an infant's plastic sippy cup, no one in the van at all. He sets Sonia on the bench in the van, steps back, and shields his eyes to look through the downpour and the wind. Where can they go? Across the street is a broad and empty lot. He turns and sees that beyond the van and the smashed-in fence and a playground is a building. It's a school.

He climbs through the space between the van and the bent wrought-iron fence and runs across the lot to a set of locked double doors. He runs back to the van, opens the gate, and pulls on the plastic latch in the floor. There, underneath, he finds the tire iron.

He runs back. He tries to wedge the iron between the doors, but it won't fit. He flips it around and smashes one of the narrow windows, uses the iron to twist and tear at the wire mesh of the safety glass. When he's made a wide enough opening, he reaches in and opens the door and props it open with the tire iron. He goes back to the van.

Sonia lies so limp, so silent as he hoists her into his arms and makes his way to the school door. Inside he feels encased in dark. Streetlights illuminate the few feet leading to a hall. The place has the familiar smell of a school, the smell of industrial cleansers and cafeteria food.

Sonia's breathing heavily. She feels light in his arms, and he's terrified as he lays her down on the floor and touches her neck to feel for her pulse. He lifts her again and walks down the hall, passing his hand along the wall, searching for a light switch. He comes to closed doors, a line of lockers. Finally he finds a switch and flips it. Fluorescent lights along the ceiling flicker and blink on.

He goes from room to room. A few are open, most are locked. He finds classroom after classroom until he comes to an office with a counter behind which he finds desks and other rooms. He darts for a phone. Holding Sonia in his arms, he dials 9-1-1, but there's no sound, no dial tone, nothing. He looks into the offices until he finds a lounge, with two sofas and three chairs around a coffee table. In the corner is a kitchenette with a sink and a refrigerator.

He lays her down on the sofa. Blood covers his arms and the front of his shirt. He sees that she has lost a lot of blood. He searches the pockets of her hoodie and finds a cell phone, flips it open, and is first heartened to see the screen light up, then dismayed to find that there are no bars, and there's no connection when he tries to dial 9-1-1.

He wants to make sure that she is stable and comfortable. He goes to the kitchenette, opens cabinet doors, the refrigerator, spies another door across the room and opens it to discover a bathroom. He goes back to the kitchen, and after a few minutes of searching there and in the office he finds a package of paper towels, a pair of scissors, and a good-size first-aid kit in a red nylon case. He goes back to the kitchen, fills a mug with water, and carries it and the kit and the scissors to where Sonia lies on the sofa. He's surprised to find that she's watching him. For a moment he's terrified because her gaze is so fixed, but she blinks, and he smiles.

"Hi," he says.

"Hi."

"You okay?"

"I'm not gonna make it."

"*Shhhh. Shhhh.*" He touches her face. "You're gonna make it. You're gonna be fine."

"I'm thirsty."

He tilts the mug to her lips. She closes her eyes and drinks. When she's done, she opens her eyes and he's startled at how dim they are, at how far away she is.

"Otto," she says.

He shakes his head. "No."

She closes her eyes. "Otto." She clenches her eyes shut. "Who was that man? Who shot at us?"

"I don't know. I saw him in Mobile. He came after me there. I think he was after Ghebelin, Hugo Ghebelin, to kill him."

"Who's Hugo Ghebelin?"

He looks at her. Her eyes are heavy, her breathing shallow. "I'll tell you, after you rest up a little bit."

She nods. He starts to rise. She grasps his arm. "Did you find it?" she says.

"Find what?"

"The deck."

He hesitates. He'd forgotten. "Maybe. I'm not sure. I found some kinda box. I just need to see what's inside."

"Mmmn."

"I'm gonna get you help. I'll go now."

She grabs his wrist tight. "Don't leave me. Please. I'm telling you I'm not gonna make it." Tears run from her eyes. "Ludwig. I'm bleeding out. I feel it. Stay with me."

"Shhh. You're gonna be okay. We just—"

"It's not where I got shot. It's something inside. I'm not gonna make it."

Ludwig takes her hand. "Okay. Okay. Just hold on, okay?"

She blinks at the ceiling. Her eyes are dull and her mouth is open. He moves his hands without purpose, clasps them together. She's stable. He's stopped the bleeding as well as he can. What can he do? There's nothing he can do.

"Ludwig?" she says.

"What is it?"

"My wallet. I need my wallet."

"Yeah. Yeah. I'll get it."

He lifts the blanket. The bottom of her shirt is black with blood. Ludwig reaches around and finds her wallet in the back pocket of her jeans. He pulls it out and finds that it's slick and grimy with her blood.

"There're pictures in it," she says. She looks at him and nods. She wants him to look, to see. He flips it open. Inside is a plastic photo folder. The first is of the girl that Ludwig saw in Mrs. S.'s house, Sonia's daughter. He glances up. Sonia nods again. He flips to the picture of a girl whose face is badly burned. The next is of a boy with bandages around his neck They are photos like the ones he remembers seeing on her bedroom wall in Landstuhl. The kids are smiling at whoever took the photo. Yet another is of a boy standing beside a bright red plastic tricycle in the driveway of what looks like a suburban house. Another is of a girl with no hair and a scarred and shattered chin. "Please. Give it to me," Sonia says.

Ludwig hands her the wallet. She clutches it in her right hand and stares at the picture of the girl. Her gaze is so intense that it reminds Ludwig of a prayer, deserving privacy. He bows his head, until he hears her sobbing and looks up.

"They could still laugh and smile," she whispers. "They *smiled* at me." She clenches the wallet closed in her hand and clasps it to her chest.

"They smiled 'cause they *liked* you," he whispers. "You were there to help them."

"No. No." She shakes her head. "They smiled 'cause they thought I was somebody else. They didn't know I was part of what hurt them. And I didn't tell them. But I knew."

She shudders and he feels it too. He knows what she means and what she feels because he had felt the same thing, over there, in the Box. He has felt it ever since. He watches her until her eyes close.

When her breathing grows heavy, Ludwig uses the scissors to cut her shirt around the wound. What he finds underneath looks mean. It looks as if an animal with a thousand teeth has taken a bite out of her shoulder and upper arm. He finds a crescent wound, half the circumference of a quarter, just below her armpit, and he wonders if a bullet or a fragment sliced deeper into her chest or abdomen. He opens the first aid kit and rifles through it, pulls out compresses, bandage rolls, wipe packets. He rips open three gauze packages and passes them over the torn and punctured skin, cleaning the gore. Sonia stirs but she doesn't wake as he dresses her wounds.

When he's done he goes to the office and checks the phone again but there's still no connection. He goes in search of a radio. With the help of the tire iron, he wrenches open a locked closet in a classroom on the far side of the building. He finds inside it nylon bags filled with soccer balls and dodgeballs and basketballs, stacks of orange traffic cones, jump ropes looped over hooks, shelves stacked with board games, and a folded inflatable kiddy pool. At the very back he finds a television on a stand. He rolls the TV down the hall to the office and plugs it in. He can get only three channels, and each is the same, covering urgent news of the region trapped in the eye of this hurricane they call Katrina. He settles on one channel and sits and watches. The storm is pummeling the coast and the city. The newscasters announce that the mayor has repeated calls for a mandatory evacuation. Questions remain about whether the levees will hold. Ludwig wonders what that means. He watches for half an hour before the television blinks off and the lights go out. He curses. Disoriented, he feels his way along the walls in the pitch black until he finds the chair beside the sofa in the lounge. He sits with Sonia's phone in his lap and listens to her breathe in her sleep.

Although the room is windowless, he can hear the storm raging, feel it buffeting the building. He's seen bad storms before, near his aunt's house in Atlanta when he was a kid and a roiling dust storm in the Box along the banks of Mileh Tharthar. But he's never seen anything quite like this. Windows in another room rattle. Ludwig imagines it could be the burned man, the burned man hunting for him, or Otto fighting to get in, struggling to live, to survive.

Ludwig climbs down from the .50-cal kit and Wonder takes his place above. He follows Vance out of the Humvee and onto the street at the east end of the bridge. A bullet-ridden, white 4Runner with flat tires stands askew in the road with its doors and hatch wide open. Blood is splattered on the inside of the open doors, smeared all over the asphalt around the wreckage. A man lies facedown farther up the road, and from the spans of the bridge above hang the naked, decimated bodies of two other men. Three Ghebelin guys kneel farther up, weapons pointed toward the far end of the bridge. The air is hot and sodden and it feels as if it is pressing down on everything.

Ludwig turns. A man lies at the base of a pale brick wall that runs alongside the road. He looks as if he's been dragged there or thrown there—however this terrible mess panned out. Ludwig runs over to help him, but he stops fast. Although the guy looks like he's screaming, no sound comes from the tortured oval of his mouth, and Ludwig sees how much blood has flowed from him and pooled around him. He turns and realizes that for all of the frenzied motion, for all of the running about of all these newly arriving marines, and the chaos and the frantic efforts to do something for these dead men, for all the commotion and panic, the moment is encased in a pulsing drone that makes Ludwig wonder if he's dreaming. Because after hours of anticipation and anxiety, and after swallowing maybe one more Go pill than he should have just half an hour earlier, he realizes that this is it and it's worse than they had described and worse than he had feared. This is Falluj—

He wakes. The cell phone shivers and buzzes in his lap. He stares at it, terrified, until he remembers that it is Sonia's phone and that it must now, somehow, by a strange miracle, be connected to the outside world. He flips it open, puts it to his ear, yells, "Hello? Hello?"

"Sonia? Sonia?" The voice is familiar.

"Missus S.——"

"Who is this?"

"Missus S. It's me. It's Ludwig." He leans forward in the chair. The relief he feels at finally talking to someone outside of the cocoon of violence and the events of the night is overwhelming. But he glances up at Sonia asleep on the sofa and feels mortified.

"Where are you? What's happening? Sonia said you were in the hospital."

"I'm fine. We're here, in New Orleans. But Sonia's hurt."

"Hurt? Hurt how? How badly is she hurt?"

Ludwig closes his eyes. He wants to lie. What can Mrs. S. do anyway but suffer helplessly up there in Connecticut? But he finds he can't do it.

"The man, the man I told you about. He was there, at the house where I thought the box might be, the deck. We were getting out and he—he shot her. He shot Sonia. She got shot in the shoulder, but I think I've got her stable. I think she's safe for now."

"For now? My goodness—"

"I need to get her to a hospital, but we can't get to one until the storm stops."

A sound comes through the line. A strangled exclamation full of grief. She starts to weep. Her panic and sorrow run through the ether that connects her phone to Sonia's.

"What happened?" she says.

"It's hard to describe. It just all went really bad really fast."

"Ludwig. Ludwig," she whispers.

Ludwig covers his other ear to better hear her.

"Is she—awake?" she asks.

"She's sleeping."

"Okay. Okay. Let her rest. My God. But when she wakes, would you do something for me?"

"Yes."

"Please let her know that I'm sorry for my lies. Tell her that for me."

"Lies? I don't—"

"You know what I mean. When we spoke before, you told me how you felt about this. I tried to argue, but—I'd told Sonia about this—this—strange talent that my mother and my grandmother had. And I wasn't lying. I told her stories of what they could do. I saw it with my own eyes. They had something—a kind of insight or intuition, like visions. Over the years I've often doubted what I saw. Was it really what I thought it was? Or were they just clever old tricks? But I lied to Sonia and Rania when I said that I had it too, that talent. I might have felt it, as a child, a kind of a feeling of a potential within me. But I never felt more than that. Later, after my family was pulled apart, all of us sent to camps, destroyed, I felt dead inside. But later, after a time, I tried to convince myself that I could do this *thing*, this foretelling. Or that with study and time, I could regain what was lost. Sonia knows how much I studied, how much I tried. She believed in me, trusted me. She believed that I was practicing some kind of great and secret art. She didn't know how desperately I searched for something that I knew in my heart was lost to us forever. And then, last night, I was so desperately afraid for Sonia that I thought I might die. I tried to hold it in. Rania is with me and I couldn't let her see how much I was panicking as I watched the hurricane on the news. Then I told Rania to go to bed and I grew frantic. I felt pains in my chest. I must have asked

Celia to give me something. Celia made me take something. I took a pill. I don't know. I can't remember. I was exhausted and afraid and I lay terrified in my bed. I must have fallen asleep. I must have taken something. I had the strangest dream. I dreamed that I was in the body of another person. I was in the body of a woman who had lived for a thousand years, maybe more. Her mind was not my mind but I could see into it—her mind. It was like visiting a strange old house. Her mind was filled with images and symbols, with a language lost to the world. Her blood ran through my veins and my blood ran through hers and I saw life in symbol, a life in which the meanings of things don't flow from what we call them but from what they are. A place where a lie is impossible because everything is laid bare and revealed in its true essence.

"And I lived a thousand years or more in a moment in the mind and blood of this strange woman. My God. It was so strange! And then I knew my time had come in this other woman's body because her body's time had come. It was time to return to myself. And I woke up with the feeling that I remembered as a child, this feeling that the truth of the world can be known, but maybe not by me. I am—not an adept. I don't know if such people exist anymore. Maybe they're all gone. And the first person I wanted to tell was Sonia, who has always believed in me although I misled her. Can you tell her that, Ludwig? Can you tell her that her aunt loves her but that her aunt isn't the woman she thinks she is? It's a lot to ask. We barely know each other. Ludwig? Ludwig, are you there? I very much need your help in this."

Ludwig clenches his eyes shut. "I'm here," he says.

He feels like an interloper. He feels as he had that day when he first met her that he is looking into her house, glimpsing the private affairs and intimacies of a family. But this time he is being asked to do so, asked not just to witness but to intercede in the business of this strange family he barely knows. And then there is Mrs. S.'s dream, which hews so close to the events of the night before that Ludwig wonders if he did in fact wake up to the sound of Sonia's phone ringing. Or maybe this is a dream within another dream?

"I'll tell her," he says.

"Thank you, Ludwig."

He hears a sound, another voice on the line. Mrs. S. says something muffled, angry.

"Hello? Hello? Sonia?"

"Who's this?" says Ludwig.

"Ludwig? Is that you? It's Celia."

Ludwig hears Mrs. S. crying in the background, a wailing complaint that breaks his heart but which slowly fades as he imagines Celia walking away from her.

"It's me. What's going on with Missus S.?"

"Oh God. It's bad here. She's been so worried about Sonia. I think she may have had a stroke. But I won't be able to get her doctor in for another hour."

"A stroke?"

"A ministroke. I think. Something's wrong. I can tell. She's been in and out."

"Jesus."

"Where are you? I thought she was trying to reach—"

The line blinks out.

"Hello? Hello?" He listens, curses. The connection's gone. The battery indicator shows the thinnest wedge of life left in the machine. He eyes the time on the screen. It is a quarter past two in the morning. He folds the phone shut, sits back, and peers through the darkness at Sonia. Mrs. S.'s words dart through his thoughts like thrown furniture. He struggles to make sense of what she said. The part about her dream makes him feel as if the world is not what he had imagined. Sonia's snoring is his only consolation. When he'd first seen her, those months ago in Landstuhl, she'd warped the air with her strange, sharp presence. But she is wounded and vulnerable lying there on the sofa. She's broken, and he wishes he could do more to help her.

He rubs his face and shuts his eyes. Otto is dead. The driver, Ghebelin, the old woman: all dead. When he'd last glimpsed it, flames were bursting from the windows of the mansion. He'd thought that he might finally trek across this desert of shadows, reach its farther edge, but he finds that he is still in it, and the black sun still fills the sky. When he opens his eyes, the room resolves itself into the moment and Sonia's breathing again draws his eyes toward her. He knows that he has to do everything he can to keep her alive.

20.

He wakes. Sonia lies still on the sofa. He listens close and hears her breathing but he doesn't hear the sounds of the storm. Is it morning? Has it ended? The cell phone is out of power. His hip flares when he tries to move. When he's able to stand, he goes to the office but the phones are still dead. From the doors through which they entered he sees branches, trash, leaves littering the playground and the street beyond. Otherwise all looks still and calm. He finds in the warm confines of the refrigerator a bag of bagels, a bag filled with shredded cheddar cheese, a carton quarter full of orange juice, half-and-half, and a jar of peanut butter. He grabs the peanut butter and a plastic spoon. Then he puts fresh water in a mug, kneels beside Sonia, and whispers her name.

She stirs from her sleep and murmurs disconnected words—*Maman—the children—we have to*—meaningless to him and intimating the past and all the things about her he doesn't know. Finally she wakes and sips the water but she won't eat the peanut butter. Her eyes are glassy, alarmingly withdrawn. His only consolation is that she looks him in the eye.

"Are you ready to go?" he says. "I'm taking you to a hospital."

She shakes her head. "I can't. I can't go. I need an ambulance."

"Okay. I'll get help. I'll get an ambulance."

"Call." She swallows. "Please."

"The phones are dead. But I'll get help."

"Fast, please."

He doesn't want to leave her there, but he has to. He stands and goes out. The air feels thin and sharp against his skin, hot but not heavy the way it's felt since he got to New Orleans or even the day before the storm. A stink, like rot and sewage, fills his nostrils. The sewers must be overrun.

He pauses at the wreckage of the car angled into the side of the pale green Dodge Caravan. The hood is crushed. What can only be shotgun blasts radiate from the center and one side of the back window. The driver-side window is halfway gone. The shattered crescent at the bottom is splashed with Sonia's blood, as are the seat, the inside of the door, and the collapsed air bag. He goes around to the passenger side and pulls open the door.

There, where he dropped it, is the small red box. He looks up and down the street, sees no one walking, no one watching. He reaches for the box and grips it tight. He'd forgotten it altogether, but now he wants it, if only to show Sonia.

When he rises, Ludwig's eye catches a familiar flash of blue, just around the corner, past the school yard and the span of iron fencing bordering its far side. He squints and sees that it's a blue Nissan. It's the burned man's car, without a doubt. He swallows, fights for a moment a visceral urge to cut and run. But the car looks empty from a distance. He looks about but the street is silent. He starts to doubt.

It could be a similar car. He understands that he has to play this carefully. His gaze traces the line of sight from the car to the wreckage, and he feels instinctively that the car is positioned as it is precisely to keep an eye on the wreckage. He takes a deep breath, slowly walks up the sidewalk, approaches gingerly, almost roundabout, scanning the quiet street, the houses across the way, the driveways and the hedges and the spaces between. As he approaches he sees that both doors on the driver side are ajar. The asphalt all along the side of the car is blackened, as if by oil. But red blood stains the doors. He looks about. The street is so quiet. Wary of leaving prints, he sets the flat of his palm against the top of the frame of the driver's door to pull it open wider. He's fearful, nauseated by the compulsion to investigate what he would rather flee from. The driver's seat and the steering wheel are stained with blood. Clothes, the burned man's coat, his hat, rest bloody and crumpled on the passenger-side seat. Ludwig looks around again, steps to the rear door, pulls it open wider.

The burned man lies facedown the length of the backseat. His shoes stick out from the car. He is shirtless. His dark gray slacks are drenched in blood. His left arm hangs limp to the floor, the barrel of the shotgun gripped in his hand. Ludwig covers his mouth and stares. An acrid stench fills the hot air. He leans in. The tattoo of a medieval knight in full armor covers the man's back. The knight is shrouded in a glowing halo or aura of fire. His helmeted head is bent as if in prayer. A long sword is held point down in his hands. Ludwig leans close to see the Gothic script that edges the blade: *My Lai - March 16, 1968*. A sour stench rises off the burned man's skin. His left side is covered with brown- and yellow-stained napkins. They litter the floor. Ludwig peers close, spying amid the gory mess the edges of ragged bullet holes in the burned man's skin.

"If only you'd backed off," Ludwig whispers.

He looks at his own tattoo, the black sun, the black hole like a wound in his soul, which he knows will never completely heal.

He backs away, turns toward the school, and breaks into a run, sprints through the halls and across the office until he kneels by Sonia's side. Very soon he understands that she's dead. Her eyes are closed and she looks peaceful. The wallet rests clenched in her hand on her chest. Ludwig takes it, looks at the picture of the girl grinning. Why is she smiling? Why are any of the children smiling, despite everything? His words of reassurance to Sonia earlier now feel hollow, like empty lies. He closes the wallet and sets it back in her hands. He covers his face and weeps, wonders if there's a place for her now, and if there is a place, is it much like the world as she knew it or the world as she wished it could be?

He waits beside her through the day and dusk. He checks the phone in the office again and again but there's no connection. He waits but no one comes. With nightfall, the presence of her perfectly still form drives him to darkest thoughts and memories. When it becomes too much, he lies on the floor out of sight of Sonia's body and falls asleep.

At some point he wakes in velvet darkness, startled by a dream in which he's trapped in a labyrinth created by the dreams of others. He fumbles for the box. Finds it on a desktop where he'd left it. For days all he'd thought about was the money Mrs. S. said she'd pay him to get the deck. He'd fantasized about it. The deck, the cards, their mystery, had been an afterthought. But now he's overwhelmed by the desire to see it, the one card, the need to know, finally, what the thing might look like if it's in the box. Without thinking, he slams the box against the edge of the desk. He doesn't know what he expects to happen, but nothing does. He bangs it again, hard. Then, for a moment, he fears he might have damaged what's inside. What if the deck is so old, it's become brittle? And what if by slamming the box, he's destroyed the cards? He might eventually open the box, but all he'll find will be dust, and he'll never know what symbol marked that last card. He sets the box down again and sits with his face in his hands, trying to remember the faces of people: Sonia's face and Otto's, and painfully, most elusive of all, Sam's.

When nightmares wake him again, he goes back to the entrance, where light streams in. He doubts at first what he sees: swirling water fills the entranceway to the top of the stairs and it is rising. He kneels and looks through the window in the door. The bottom half of the playground set, the fence, the path, and the street beyond are all sub-merged under black water for as far as he can see. *My God*, he says. A river flows where the street was only hours before. The car they crashed has vanished, but he can see the roof of the minivan. The water runs fast and the things borne on it—leaves, branches, plastic bags, and garbage, a torrent of filth, rush by. The air is hot and stinks of sewage and rot.

Ludwig hears voices outside, the sound of water splashing. He climbs down the stairs into the water up to his waist and out the door. There, just beyond the minivan, two men, one white, one black, row a long yellow rowboat up the street.

"Hey," calls Ludwig. He wades to the fence.

The men look this way and that before they spot him. They push their paddles into the water and turn about in the current.

"Hey," the black man calls out. He has on a sky-blue baseball cap and aviator glasses.

"What the fuck happened?" says Ludwig.

"Crazy, huh?" says the white guy.

"Fuckin' nuts," says the black guy.

"But where'd all this come from?"

"Levees broke."

"Levees?"

"Levees on the lake. They all broke. All the water's poured into the city. It's a total mess."

"Jesus." Ludwig can't fathom it. He doesn't know what any of it means. "Where you goin'?" he asks.

"Downtown."

"Is it all flooded?"

"Far as we know, yeah."

"Jesus. Listen, guys. I need some help here."

"Whattya need?"

"A friend of mine. She got into an accident the other night and she got hurt real bad."

"Hospital's all shut down, buddy. How hurt is she?"

Ludwig hesitates. He feels hopeless. "She's dead," he says. He wishes he could control it, but his voice is cracked and jagged. He can't hold back his tears. "She was hurt, and I was headed to a hospital, but she died."

The men stare at him.

"Where is she?" says the black guy.

"She's inside."

"Inside the school there?"

"That's right."

The white man leans toward the other man and they confer. Finally they look at him.

"Sorry, man," says the white guy. They start to row. "We can't help you."

"Please."

"Just sit still, brother," says the black guy. "Wait it out. She's better off here, with you."

Ludwig wades deeper into the water, stumbles.

"Stay away," he hears the other man say. They paddle quickly away with the current, down the street. The white guy in the back of the boat looks back once, twice, and not again as Ludwig watches them vanish into the distance.

Through the day the water continues to rise until the halls of the school are submerged in it. The water enters the office, curves around the furniture. He puts the box in a plastic bag and sits beside it on a desk. When the water keeps rising, he wraps the loose end of the bag around his fist and goes to where Sonia is. Her body is stiff when he lifts her. He wades through the water and takes her up the hall and up a flight of steps and sets her down on a landing beneath a boarded window.

She lies so still. The heat and the terrible humidity make it worse. He stands for a moment in silence with his hands over his mouth, weeping and cringing. He kneels beside her and begs for her forgiveness.

After, in the bathroom, Ludwig tries to clean his hands but the residue of death and guilt won't come off. He rubs harder and harder to no avail. He shudders and curses himself. He feels breathless, fugitive, brimming with shame and guilt. How can things have come to this? Why did he let things go this far?

In the afternoon he decides to go. He goes to where her body lies, bearing a length of heavy curtain he has pulled down from one of the office windows. He sets the bag with the box on the floor. He sets her on the curtain and takes her wallet in hand. He looks at the photos, eyes the smiling children with a great wariness, as if they can see him, as if they can see what has happened to Sonia. He pulls out her driver's license and three of the photos. He leaves her Army ID, the credit cards, and the photos of most of the children, including her daughter.

Then he puts the wallet in her pocket and wraps her carefully in the moss-green cloth, sits and weeps and watches her shrouded body.

He goes to the equipment closet down the hall, rummages until he finds a tire pump, and pulls out the folded inflatable pool. He unfurls the pool in the hall and pumps it till it's taut. The outer edge is adorned with pictures of cartoon flowers and little blue and pink and yellow songbirds. After, he wraps Sonia's photos and her license along with the box in a black plastic garbage bag. He carries the pool and wades into the street. He's afraid of getting electrocuted. How does it work with the electrical wires? If they're submerged in the water, could that mean that a current running through could hit him?

When he's in the street, he sets the pool in the water. It jerks fast and Ludwig grabs it. He climbs on and lies down and it starts to move fast. The current runs strong and it takes him up the street. He blinks and turns. He doesn't know where the current is bearing him. He holds tight to the bundled bag. The air is hot and acrid and the sky is a deep blue wall above him. The water sweeps him down the middle of the street, past houses, storefronts, all half submerged under the thick brown water.

He comes to a curve and a crossroads in the current. Ahead, he sees the downtown—tall buildings, the silver crescent of the Superdome. He turns in a moment of panic, wonders whether the channel headed north and south will sweep him off his course, but the current pulls him toward the city, toward the distant buildings, away from the late-afternoon sun.

21.

The man and the woman at the banquet table do a good job of not
looking put out. It's the trash bag, Ludwig knows, and maybe the
smell, after the swimming, after the days at the evacuation center and
after the long bus ride north. He has not had a chance to shower
or shave in days. But this high school is taking in people fleeing the
aftermath of the hurricane. As Ludwig follows the man to an indoor
basketball court lined with cots, he asks if he can use a phone to make
a call.

"You can, but the office is closed for the night. You can call first
thing in the morning, at seven thirty."

He takes a shower and has dinner in the cafeteria with a couple
dozen other people. A few of them talk about what they've been
through, strange and surreal tales of survival. Others, including
Ludwig, eat and listen in a state of weary stupefaction. After, someone
wheels in a television. Every channel carries news of New Orleans.
Nine days have passed since that violent night. Now he is in Meridian,

Mississippi, a survivor, some kind of refugee. It feels like a lifetime ago. At least, Ludwig sees on the TV, the military is there in full force. The officer he'd pleaded with at the National Guard station had told him that the address he'd provided would help them find Sonia's body. But after someone switches off the television and Ludwig sacks out on his cot he stares at the ceiling and feels anxious and full of doubt. He sees the rolled-up curtain, her shroud, whether his eyes are open or shut tight.

When he wakes, it's morning. He showers in the boys' locker room and asks to use a phone.

"Hello."

"Hi. It's Ludwig."

"Oh. Oh, Ludwig," says Celia. "Where are you?"

"I'm in Meridian, in Mississippi."

"Thank God. Oh God. We've been so worried. Is Sonia okay?"

"Celia— Celia—" He wants to say it. He's prepared to say it, but the words keep stopping. "Sonia's dead."

"What?"

"She—she didn't make it."

"Oh my God."

Ludwig hears Celia breathing and a muffled, hesitant sound.

"Celia. I'm so sorry, Celia. Are you there?"

She starts to sob.

"I tried to get her to a hospital, but I couldn't— She— I just—"

"Oh my God. What happened?"

"She got shot, in the shoulder. Maybe her side. I couldn't move her, and I was going to get help but— She didn't make it." He shudders, closes his eyes, covers his shut eyes with his palm. "She bled to death."

Celia weeps. "I don't know how to tell Missus S."

"I can tell her."

"How will I tell Rania?"

"I can help you tell them."

"No, no. I have to. I have to do it. Oh God. I'll tell her. She's just been sick. I mean, sicker than usual."

"Is she okay?"

"She's really sick, but she's strong. Where are you? Are you okay?"

"I'm at this place, this school they've set up for the evacuation. I'm trying to figure out how to get back home."

"Is there anything I can do?"

"No, I just need to find a ride up. There might be a bus or a train leaving tomorrow."

"Are you coming here?"

"I want to."

"Yes, come. Call if you can or just come."

"Okay."

"Ludwig, get home safe. Call if you need anything."

"Okay."

She hangs up.

Ludwig sets the phone down. He goes to an exit door that lets onto the parking lot behind the school. The day is rising. The blue sky vaults above Meridian. He stares out at it and he repeats the name, his boy's, like a chant: *Sam. Sam. Sam.*

22.

Ludwig wakes, startled, and watches the quiet suburbs and the woods pass. Fall will come soon, he sees. The leaves have lost their luster. Just before noon he climbs off the train in Stamford, Connecticut.

———

He didn't call back after they spoke three days before, but he feels as if Celia has been waiting for him. She casts open the dining room curtains just as he approaches and opens the door just as he's about to knock. He's surprised when she hugs him.

"C'mon in. Come in. You look exhausted."

"I'm okay."

"But you've traveled so far. Are you hungry? Would you like some coffee? Tea?"

"Coffee, thanks."

He follows her across the front hall. He expects that she'll turn right, into the dining room in which he first met Mrs. S., but Celia instead heads down the hall, to the kitchen. He follows her to the sunroom door, beyond which he sees Mrs. S. seated on a sofa in a nest of fluffy blankets. A lanky young girl of about thirteen or fourteen sits on a chair adjacent reading a book. Ludwig can see that it is Sonia's daughter. He blinks. The girl looks so much like her mother that he wants to turn and leave as quickly as he can. He can't face her. "Jesus," he whispers.

Celia grasps his arm. "I know. I know."

"Rania? Right?"

"Yes."

"Does she know?"

"Yeah. She knows. Both of them know. Missus S.—she didn't say a word. She seemed to—I don't know how to describe it. It was like watching someone wilt all of a sudden. Rania cried and cried and Missus S. just held her. I don't know if either of them have slept since I told them."

Ludwig breathes deep and shakes his head. He glances beyond the girl, beyond the sunroom glass where leaves scurry across the grass. The sight chills him. Celia pushes open the sliding door and a wave of heat wraps him in the room's embrace. Ludwig follows her into the sunroom.

As he approaches, Mrs. S. looks up, expressionless, with unseeing eyes. She raises her hand and gestures for him to sit on the sofa across the table from her, and he does.

"Hi," Ludwig says.

The young girl frowns. "Hello," she says. She sets her book on the floor beside the chair, tucks her hands beneath her thighs, and watches him.

This isn't what he had expected. None of this is what he envisioned or planned for as he had traveled up from Meridian. What did he expect? He did not expect Sonia's daughter to be there. And he hadn't expected Mrs. S. to have changed as much as she has. She looks old, as ageless as Mrs. G. had looked in her deathbed in that house in New Orleans. When he'd first met Mrs. S., she'd told him she was sick. Ludwig wonders what has happened to the heart monitor. He wonders if she's so far gone that she doesn't need it anymore.

"I'll get coffee," says Celia. As she steps back into the kitchen and closes the sliding door behind her, Ludwig watches her with a feeling of abandonment bordering on resentment.

He leans back and sinks into the sofa. The room is silent and humid. Mrs. S. looks small and wizened, not at all like the vital priestess of his memory. It's hard to imagine that the woman whose eyes now blindly graze his face back and forth, back and forth is the same woman who downed a tumblerful of whiskey only weeks ago.

"You're Mister Mason," says the girl.

He nods. "Ludwig."

"You're a friend of my mom's."

"Yes." He hesitates. "And you're Rania."

"Yeah." She stares at him. Finally, "So my *Bebe* hired you—to, to look for something for her?"

"Bebe?"

"My great-aunt."

"Yeah," Ludwig says. "That's right."

She squints at him. "And something bad happened. My mother was with you. My mother got hurt, and she—she's dead?"

Ludwig's mouth dries in an instant. He blinks, nods, sits up on the edge of the sofa. "Yes."

"What happened? What happened to my mom?"

When his voice comes, he can't control it. It trembles and his hands shake in his lap. "Are you sure——? Maybe your great-aunt——"

"Please tell us," says Mrs. S. "Tell us everything."

Ludwig and Rania turn toward Mrs. S.

The girl rises. "*Bebe*—" she whispers, as she sits next to her great-aunt and leans into the older woman's arms.

Mrs. S. strokes Rania's face. "She knows some things," she says. "But she should know everything. I know it's a lot to ask, but you were there, Ludwig, please. I only know what Celia told me. That's all I've been able to tell Rania. Tell us. Tell us what happened."

Rania stares at him. Ludwig swallows and looks away. He looks at the bag on the cushion beside him. He picks it up and sets it on the table in front of him and stares at it. What is he to do? What can he do but what he first set out to do? He's gone too far—to New Orleans and back—to go back now.

"I did what you asked," he says. He tells them about Mobile and the empty house and the burned man. He tells them what he discovered about the Ghebelin family, and their strange history in the world of the occult. He describes his encounter with the burned man, the ride west of Mobile, his escape, the ride to New Orleans and the events that took place there, to the night of the hurricane.

When he gets to the part about the mayhem and the murders in the house, about Hugo Ghebelin and Ghebelin's grandmother and Otto, he treads with caution. As he describes the last moments of the old woman, Mrs. G., on that terrible night, he watches Mrs. S.'s face. But neither her blank eyes nor her passive face betray any reaction. Could it be that the dream Mrs. S. had described had some connection to what he saw that night in New Orleans? When he describes Sonia's last day, his words become slow and deliberate. Rania stares at him wide-eyed. She sobs softly, moans and claws and nuzzles into her *bebe*'s embrace.

"I had to leave her," he says, with more bitterness than he'd intended. "I had to get out while I could. I'm so, so sorry." He looks at Mrs. S. and feels a surge in his chest, anger mixed with a sudden suspicion that she may have known all along the price that would be paid. But then he remembers his own part in it: his heedlessness, his recklessness, his choice in the matter.

By the time he reaches this moment, now, the part of the story in which he pulls the box out of the bag and sets it before Mrs. S. and Rania, just as he had promised, it has started to rain. He watches the rain, he waits, he thinks and wonders aloud, more to himself than to them, "Who was the burned man?"

"The deck must always have a wild card," says Mrs. S. "There must always be a space for the chaos in our hearts. Always."

"I don't understand. When you called that night of the storm, you said you didn't believe—"

"I didn't say I didn't believe. I said I doubted. There is a difference. Most people look for certainty in most things. They want to know with absolute certainty and confidence the facts of the human heart. But to seek certainty in human affairs is a game of fools and fanatics." Her eyes are fixed on him. She smiles, but her eyes are filled with mourning. "Open it," she says.

He expected this. He leans forward, picks up the box. "I can't," he says.

She frowns. "Rania, will you look?"

Rania rises and reaches across and takes it. He watches her study it, eyeing each side. Finally she kneels on the floor beside the table. "You told me—" She presses her thumbs against the handles. The top drawer springs open. He looks up. *Of course*, he thinks. She sets the box on the table.

"See what's inside," says Mrs. S.

Rania reaches in, pulls out wads of densely packed paper. She unravels it, finds inside the paper yet another bundle of paper. She sets it on the table.

"Open it," says Mrs. S.

Rania hesitates, leans forward, unwraps the bundle to reveal a tiny deck, with cards only as tall as her index finger. Their backs are covered with ornate designs—patterns, almost Islamic, of crimson and green and gold.

"Give them to me," says Mrs. S.

Rania hands her great-aunt the deck. Mrs. S. holds it, as if testing its balance and weight. Her joints look stiff and bent, but she shuffles the cards with mesmerizing ease. They flow like quicksilver through her fingers, as if they had always been meant for her. She starts to set them on the table in that way Ludwig remembers, three small piles: the past, the present, and the future. She is reading his fortune.

The first time she'd stopped because he had wanted her to, because the path looked bleak. He'd seen nothing for himself but days shadowed by hopelessness and dark, all leading to a seemingly absolute and inevitable darkness. But now he sees it: a way in the world, a way toward light and life. He nods. Why not? Who can tell him the way now? So when she prompts him, he reaches out with his left hand and turns over the past, turns over the present, and finally reaches for the one that won't set his destiny but will only suggest options, choices—the final card, the last.

Acknowledgements

Flocie Lohier
Raymond Lohier
Udaya Nallamothu
Satya Nallamothu
Raymond Lohier Jr.
Donna Lee

Jocelyn Sterlin
Reynold Sterlin
Natalie Sterlin
Regine Sterlin Jeune
Florence Sterlin
Jovelt Jeune
Balajee Nallamothu
Tammy Nallamothu
Shivajee Nallamothu
Terri Nallamothu
Brahmajee Nallamothu
Padma Nallamothu

Josette Beliard
Martine Joseph
Vanezza Laudé
Georges Bédard
Karine Léger

Michel Ambroise
James Ambroise

Francois Elder Thebaud
Patricia Thebaud

Michael Den Tandt
Yvonne Joyner Levette
Andrew Levette

Venkat Polavarapu
Deepa Polavarapu

Swarupa Anila
Vincent G C Anicca
Sunita Rao

Ashley Bruce
Peter Tashjian
Ashley Tashjian
Alan Davison

Francesco Duina
Angela Atkinson Duina
David Schab
Ariel Kaminer
Andrew Blom
Lisa Ceglia

Matt Wise
Kate Imel
Colby Groves

Doug Seibold
Marla Seibold
Andy Winston
Peter McGuigan
Richie Kern

Peter O'Leary
Rebecca Houze
Michael O'Leary
Una Moon
Jim Pollock
Esme Codell
Regina Silvia A. Sant'Anna
Doug Skytes
Carmine Cervi
Laurie Little
Michael Quattrocki
Angela Quattrocki
Marcelo Ferrer
Sarah Muir Ferrer
Mike McMahon

Lisa Klink
Diana Renn

Elaine Bright
Jeffrey Rouse
David McLaughlin
Beverley Koven
Jennifer Franklin

Stephen Chester
Charles McLandress
Diane Pendlebury
Nick Radia
Kiera Vanderlugt
Jeff Newman
Julie King
Dan Bender
Jo Sharma
Chris Mason
Charlotte Mason
Donna Bailey Nurse
Jefferson Nurse
Molly Peacock
Michael Groden
Agnès van't Bosch
Graham Dudley
Lawrence Hill
Miranda Hill

Caldera
Canada Council for the Arts
Ontario Arts Council
Toronto Arts Council